SUNBROOK MANSION

BED AND BREAKFAST
of
romance, elegance, and mystery

Adult Fiction

by

CYNTHIA TAYLOR BILLOTTE

Cover and art elements created
by Denice Rodaniche

 Published by AzBukiVeri LLC,
Publishing agency

azbukiveri@gmail.com

ISBN: 978-1-7350079-3-9

For my Mother

Your last words to me

"Cynthia, my little girl."

I shall cherish them forever.

Acknowledgments

I must begin by thanking my family because I love them. They persuaded me to follow my writing dream and to "stop talking about it and get to work on that novel." Thank you David, Gwen, Ike and Corinne Taylor, Latifah Walsh, Carrie Ann, Don, Eric and Bradly Hicks, Andrew, Wendy and Morgen Taylor. Thank you, Daddy, George (Geno) Taylor, for reading my early short stories and touting how good they were even when they weren't. I know, that's the special relationship of a father and his daughter. You're gone now, and I miss you madly! Thank you Mom, Jeanie Taylor, for calling and telling me about the writing class ad in the Altoona Mirror that ended up leading me to the Altoona Writer's Guild and the means to finish this book. (This was the second time you saved my life.) I wish you were here. I miss you every day. Thank you Cousin Angela Haubert, I still may not have written a word if it wasn't for your encouragement to join you in the NaNoWriMo challenge. Thank you Cousins Louise Pence, Mary Ann Lacy, and Bridget Lacy-Wolak, along with my lovely friends Sandra Billotte and Robin Ritchey for telling me you enjoyed reading an early draft, grammar mistakes and all.

Many thanks to all my fellow writers, published authors and poets of the Altoona Writer's Guild. Especially, Janet Vilke, Rose McConehey, *What's not to love,* Sue Partenheimer, *Caster Oil Rig Tales,* Marsena Fickes, Rodger Johnson, Denice Rodaniche, Brent Filer, Nancy Head, *Restoring the Shattered,* Dan Dusza and Norma Smith, *The Woods*. I know sometimes I just didn't get it, but you whipped me into writing shape chapter by chapter through many years of meetings and emails. Thank you for your kind critiques, even when my writing was laughable. Thank you for your encouragement when my confidence waivered. You all held me up with a gentle prompting that I could write this book to the end – and that my story did matter. Thank you, Norma Smith, for volunteering your time to meticulously proofread the manuscript when I didn't know where to turn. Thank you Denice Rodaniche, for the amazing painting for my book cover – your talent perfectly captured the enchantment of Sunbrook Mansion. And a special thanks, in the memory of our late teacher, Robert Broadwater, whose inspiration knew no limits.

Thank you, Adelina, my publisher, for choosing my novel. It has been a pleasure meeting you, my friend. Thank you for working so hard going back and forth with me via email to get it into shape.

To Michael, our wonderful son, who has been a special blessing from God, we are thankful and love you more and more every day. Thank you for always being available to print my last-minute rewrites right before my writer's meetings.

And finally, thank you to my husband, Mike, the man of my dreams!

Contents

Author's Note

This is a work of fiction. Nothing in the narrative is absolutely true, with the exception of the historical figure, John Lloyd. It is loosely based on my experience as owner and proprietor of my bed and breakfast, and my partnership of a consignment shop with my mother and sister-in-law. It encompasses the breath and life of my remarkable time, blessed with the romance, contentment, and joy of living in an enchanting historical home.

Chapter 1

All my dreams came true at Sunbrook Mansion; dreams of sharing love, happiness, friendship, and success. Sunbrook wasn't stingy with fulfilling dreams because it enchanted everyone who stayed within its walls. Sunbrook also possessed secrets; secrets that it revealed slowly, in its own time. It would divulge a secret, only when needed, and when one was resigned to accept.

***

My first guests to stay at Sunbrook would be coming down to breakfast soon. I had spent the morning baking cinnamon rolls, cutting fruit and mixing up pancake batter. My last chore before they'd appear was to set the dining room table. I laid the white linen napkin on the antique white, Irish lace tablecloth, to the left of the new, teal and white china plate. My hand trembled as I held up the crystal goblet to check for spots, before lowering it to its proper place, the upper right of the plate. My confidence wavered. "Can I really do this," I said aloud to no one, but a faint voice in my ear quipped, "you…can."

Not sure if the words were my own—they still had the same effect. I straightened my back and raised my head in defiance, chasing the negativity from my mind. The stance reminded me of my surroundings.

I smiled as my eyes took in Sunbrook's large, opulent dining room. Cobalt blue wall panels with white trim surrounded me. I looked up and admired two intricate stained glass windows above the panels. They hung opposite each other competing to spread the morning light artfully around the room, as if proud of their colors. The large glistening chandelier, dripping in crystal, dazzled for attention above the center of the room. A massive, blue-tiled fireplace stood at one end and a bank of leaded glass windows at the other where the sun streamed through, flooding the room with light. I closed my eyes, took a moment to bask in its warmth, and then sighed in my bliss. My shoulders dropped, and my back relaxed. I resumed my task, picked up a glimmering fork, inspected it for fingerprints, and then set it, with a pat for perfect, on top of the folded napkin. I had just finished as my guests were coming down the stairs. I rushed through the butler's pantry to the kitchen where Grace, my assistant, stood at the stove tilting a ladle, dripping pancake batter onto the griddle beside a line of sizzling bacon.

"They're coming," I whispered. I pulled the crystal pitcher of orange juice and fruit plate I had prepared earlier out of the refrigerator and then placed them on a large tray. I hurried across the kitchen and grabbed the platter of cinnamon rolls warming in the oven and added it to the tray.

"Calm down, Tiffany," Grace said. "Everything will be ready as soon as you come back from serving the food your holding."

My guests were in town to attend the first Penn

State game of the season. They played Wisconsin last night and lost. There were a total of ten fans from both teams. It proved easier to serve them all at one table, so I set them up together. I didn't realize that it could be a problem until Grace brought it to my attention.

"They're rivals. Didn't you think it would be uncomfortable for them to face each other let alone share a table for breakfast," she said.

"Oh, I didn't think of that."

"Didn't think so."

"Oh no, it's too late to set up another table." I stood frozen like a Christian awaiting persecution and predicted in my head their whole reprimand and refusal to sit together.

"Stop that," Grace said, interrupting my mind rant.

I jumped, which brought my thoughts back to the kitchen.

"With those wide eyes, I knew you were off on one of your, *'How could I be so stupid'* or *'I should have known'*." She mocked me, miming quotes in the air with her fingers, and then put her hands on her hips, "Did they beat you up, too?"

"No," I said in a small voice, embarrassed by her observation.

"Just relax and serve the coffee. They'll be more upset if it's late. We could have an all-out brawl if they don't get their caffeine. Now take a deep breath."

I followed her command, heaved a breath in, let it out, and waited for more direction.

"Now go," she said, scooping her hands toward the dining room as if pushing me on.

I gathered my courage and sailed through the dining room door, tray in hand.

"Good morning," I said in my most cheerful energetic voice.

I set the matching white coffee butlers on each end of the table. My eyes swept the room as I walked around again with two sets of the juice, fruit and cinnamon rolls. Two couples were standing in front of the windows looking out, while two were at the other end admiring the fireplace, and one couple hadn't come down yet.

They all mumbled their greetings as they gathered around the table, looking down at it as if contemplating what to do next.

"Please, have a seat," I said, making a wide gesture down the table with my hand. "Sit wherever you like."

Everyone pulled out the chair in front of them at the same time and sat, like robots all programmed in the same sequence.

"Please, help yourself."

One gentleman smiled at everyone, "Hello, I'm Joel and this is my wife Annie." He caressed the shoulder of the petite, blond on his left. He picked up the coffee butler, poured his wife's cup and then his own before passing it on to the person beside him.

"Hi, I'm Gene and this is my wife Joan." The rest followed with their introductions and the tension seemed to leave the room.

"The cinnamon rolls are warm, so eat up. I'll be

back soon with pancakes and bacon."
I entered the kitchen to a spread of plates heaped high with steaming hot pancakes and crisp bacon, along with two bowls of peach and blueberry glaze and four small pitchers of maple syrup, all sitting under the warming lights waiting to be served. Grace sat at the table, leaning back in her chair, gazing out the window. She took a lazy sip from her steaming mug of coffee.

"The guests haven't checked out yet. How can you be so calm?" I asked. Then, rushed around the counter to the refrigerator and pulled out two crystal bowls of fresh whipped cream. I set them on a tray and added the fruit glazes and syrup to serve before the pancakes.

Without taking her eyes away from the window, she just pushed out her arm, her hand waving me away. I let out an exasperating breath, picked up the tray and raced to the dining room. The guests were eating and conversing like old friends. I didn't pay attention to what they were talking about, just smiled and passed the bowls from the tray to the table and removed the empty dishes, as discreetly as possible, then retreated to the kitchen. They were talking football when I returned with the main course.

"We needed that first down," Gene said.

"Yeah, we got some good breaks… oh, they look delicious," Joel said. He drove the serving fork into the stack and balanced four pancakes onto his plate. He passed them on and added four strips of bacon, before adding two spoonful of peaches, a generous pour of maple syrup, and then topped it all off with a large dollop of whipped cream. "But both teams played a good game."

"How gracious Joel is," I thought. What a difference in how the actual morning had unfolded as opposed to my original scenario. I strolled back to the kitchen delighted with the outcome.

I waited a half hour for them to enjoy their breakfast before going back in carrying my guest book. I laid it by Joel and started to remove their dishes, "If you don't mind, I would appreciate it if everyone would sign my guest book before you leave. All comments are welcomed."

After all the guests checked out happy, some with plans to return for an extended stay, I strode into the kitchen.

"Here take this," Grace handed me a steaming cup of tea. "You look pleased but a bit frazzled. Sit down and relax. Everything is cleaned up here; I'm going upstairs and start on the rooms." Not waiting for a reply, she turned, rushed out to the foyer and bounded up the stairs. I marveled at her energy.

Relieved to sit awhile, I settled into the chair, propping my feet on the seat across from me. I brought the cup to my lips and took a sip. The sweet warm liquid soothed my soul as it went down. I sank further into the chair to reflect and found myself wishing my husband, Mike, were here. The phone on the table in front of me rang, startling me from my reverie. I answered; my ear tingled at the sound of Mike's voice. "Did they leave yet?"

"Yes," I said.

"Well, how'd it go?"

"Wonderful, they all left satisfied with their stay. They wrote nice comments in my guest book."

"Good, glad to hear it. I'm happy for you, Tiffany. You'll probably have more football fans stay for future Penn State home games. I assume you like football now."

"I love it," I said. Then, punched my fist into the air and cheered, "Home Run!"

Guest Book Comments

"A-1. Excellent! Other than we lost to Wisconsin."
"Sunbrook was icing on the cake of the Wisconsin victory!"

Chapter 2

After relishing in my morning success, I drank the last of my tea and deposited my cup in the sink, before going upstairs to help Grace change the bed sheets. Catching my reflection in the mirror, I smiled and said, "You did it!"

"You...did," a voice whispered in my ear that sounded like the same encouraging resonance from this morning. I jerked around searching for the source, but the room was empty. Shaking my head in dismissal, I walked out to the foyer and climbed the stairs. I slid my hand up the ebony, oak railing with each step, enjoying its smoothness beneath my palm. I lingered on the landing and then sat on the long, built-in oak bench behind me, delighted by the colorful light show that the wide span of Tiffany windows cast on the stairs and the vestibule above. My fingers swirled back and forth across the wine cushion beneath me, reveling in the luxury of the soft plush velvet.

After a few minutes, I heard Grace moving about in the Trust room. Reluctantly, I abandoned my moment of pleasure and climbed the remaining stairs, maneuvering around a mountain of sheets destined for the wash. I observed Grace sliding the corner of the bottom sheet onto the mattress and hurried around to the other side to help her.

"I'm impressed that you have all the beds stripped and disinfected."

"Yeah, stripping is easy for me." Grace stood and shimmied her body as if dancing for dollars. Then, she bent back over and resumed her task. "But I'm glad you're here to help make them up again."

I chuckled at her risqué dance display. "Well, I'm glad to help. You make it fun."

After we finished making all the beds, we went downstairs, prepared soup and sandwiches, and sat down for lunch.

"It will take me the rest of today to finish unpacking and decorating the master bedroom. I'll start working on it right after lunch," I said.

"No problem! I think I'll start painting the ceiling in the third floor bathroom."

We both worked into the evening, only stopping for supper. The clock in the foyer struck ten. I heard Grace's footsteps on the stairs before she popped her head in through the doorway. "Ready for a cup of tea?" she asked.

"You bet. I'm done here."

"Looks great," she said, surveying the room.

"Thank you. Let's go. I need a break." We both headed down to the kitchen.

"Mm, chamomile, every muscle in my body feels relaxed," I said after taking a few sips.

"I agree." Grace had downed half of hers already. She does everything on rapid speed. "Don't be alarmed if you hear any noise in the middle of the night. Sometimes I have trouble sleeping and have to get up and walk around. I might even do a little work. I'll try to be quiet, so I don't wake you," she said.

"Ok, but I'm so tired I don't think anything would wake me. We accomplished a lot today. I think we'll be ready for next weekend's guests. Although, the closer the day comes, the more nervous I get. I hope everything goes well and they enjoy their stay here."

"I know they will. Don't worry, we'll make sure everything's ready," she said.

Grace was a great support as well as an efficient assistant.

"Well, my tea is empty; time to spend my first night at Sunbrook," I said. "Goodnight Grace."

I climbed the stairs to the landing and sat on the bench, like I had done earlier. The absence of daylight and the soft radiance from the moon-globe pendant light gave the foyer below and the vestibule a mysterious glow, their nook and crannies filled with shadows. I admired the view, drinking in the experience with the revelation that Sunbrook belonged to me. I savored the moment before climbing the last few stairs to my room.

I took my time with my nightly ritual and then tucked myself into the king-size brass bed that Mike and I would share in our enchanting, new home. The fresh, tawny sheets felt like satin on my skin and the fluffy, down comforter warmed my body. I snuggled in and drifted off to dreams of beautiful brides descending the staircase to be united with their one and only - until a noise from above woke me. I listened for a moment and then realized that Grace must not have been able to sleep and decided to paint the ceiling in the room over mine. I heard the pan rattle as she pushed the roller across it, soaking in the paint; then, a few minutes of silence before I heard the roller in the pan again. I listened in the darkness until the repetition lulled me back to sleep.

***

Grace was already in the kitchen, sitting at the table drinking coffee, when I came down, "Good morning, Grace."

"Good morning," she said and took a gulp from her mug with a big "G" monogram.

I spied the pot on the counter and filled my own cup before sitting across from her.

"Mm, coffee's good. You made it just right, Grace."

"Thanks. I thought it tasted pretty good too, but the expensive coffee maker had more to do with it than I did."

"Did you have trouble sleeping last night?"

"I slept better last night than I have in a long time."

"You mean you weren't painting on the third floor in the middle of the night? A noise overhead woke me."

"Wasn't me. Are you sure you weren't dreaming?"

"No, I'm positive I heard it. How strange. You don't think we have a ghost, do you?"

"Well, we could go up and see if the painting is done," she said.

We rushed up the stairs. Grace entered the room first. "Ah darn, everything is as I left it. I guess I'll have to finish the room after all."

"Well, I'm relieved it's not a ghost. There must be some other explanation for what I heard last night because I'm certain that I was awake and heard something."

"We'll figure it out. Now no more talk of ghosts," she said, her eyes darting around the room.

"Maybe you'll hear it too and we can investigate," I left the room and was halfway down the narrow staircase when Grace yelled.

"Hey, wait for me!" She darted past me almost knocking me down.

Guest Book Comments

"Just beautiful, we really enjoyed our stay!"

Chapter 3

"I booked an anniversary couple in the bridal chamber, with extras, for tonight. They're checking in at three o'clock."

"Ok, I'll get it ready." Grace said.

"After the call ended, I recognized the name and realized the bride is an old colleague, so it's important that everything is perfect."

"Well, nothing's perfect. You worry too much. It's a great house. A great place to celebrate, it'll be all right," she said and then bounced up the stairs to prepare the room.

"Well, I hope for perfect anyway," I said under my breath, so she didn't hear. Grace is opinionated, and I have yet to win an argument with her.

I grabbed a clean dust cloth from the cupboard. But she's also a hard worker, and a good and caring person who is quick to help out her family and friends, without complaint.

She's right about Sunbrook, it is a perfect setting for any celebration, I mused while polishing up the staircase railing. I caressed each spindle with every swipe of the soft flannel cloth. I never tire of polishing the rich, dark wood to a vibrant sheen. I'm blessed to live and run a business in such a beautiful home.

The guests were set to arrive soon, so I rushed

up the stairs to shower and dress. The Westminster chimes of the antique clock in the foyer filled the house with its soothing melody. I waited in anticipation for it to calm my frazzled nerves, but it didn't help. I did a quick check of my makeup in the vanity mirror and then wandered through each room making sure everything was spotless, with nothing out of place. The doorbell rang. I took a deep breath and opened the door.

"Hello and welcome! I'm Tiffany. Please come in." Mary hadn't changed much since we worked together on the *Out Of the Darkness* suicide prevention a decade ago. Her dark brown hair was still shoulder length, and there were a few fine lines around her mouth, but her striking sapphire blue eyes still captured her youth.

"Hi," Mary said smiling, a look of recognition crossed her face as they stepped through the door. "Well, hello Tiffany. It's nice to see you again. This is my husband, Nick."

"Hello," he said with a half-smile. Nick was tall with a slender build. He was quite handsome with short, light-brown hair, hazel eyes, narrow straight nose and full mouth. He stood close to Mary with his right side slightly behind her and matched her steps as if following her lead.

"How beautiful," Mary said when they walked further into the foyer. She marveled at the ornate oak panels that climbed half way up all four walls and the tapestry above the fireplace. She ran her hands down one of the four pillars that flanked the library and music room doorways. "The rooms are so large, but I feel so warm and cozy."

"Yes, I know what you mean. It's like the house caresses you," I said, thrilled with her glowing smile. Nick still stood near Mary, with his hands behind his back looking all around. He had a look of interest on his face, but made no comment. "Come, I'll show you where I'll be serving breakfast."

They followed me through the library and into the large blue and white dining room.

"Oh, how lovely! It's so bright, and oh, so elegant," Mary said.

"Yes, the wall of leaded glass windows allows in a lot of light."

She looked back at Nick, "Breakfast will be special, won't it, Nick?" He looked down at her and said, "Yes, it will."

That is when I got the feeling it was Mary's idea to spend their anniversary at a local B&B and Nick came here for her. Dinner out would have been enough celebrating for him. Intimidated by his reaction and wanting this to end, I said, "I'll show you to your room now."

My shoulders dropped with relief when Mary replied, "Yes, it is time to get ready for dinner. We have reservation at Finelli's at 5:00 and tickets for *Ghost Show* at the Mishler Theater."

"That sounds like a wonderful evening. I think *Ghost Show* is over at 9:00. Your champagne will be chilling in your room when you return."

"Great," Mary said. Nick just nodded in agreement.

My self-confidence began to waver. It calmed

me to know I didn't have to encounter them again until breakfast. As soon as they disappeared upstairs, I went into the kitchen and let out a ragged breath.

Grace sat at the table staring out the window. She must have been listening to our exchange. "She sounded excited to be here. I watched them arrive. They look like a nice couple. Boy, is he handsome!"

I crossed the kitchen and joined her at the table. "Yes he is, but I don't think he wants to be here, he doesn't seem impressed at all."

"There you go again, worrying about whether they're happy here or not. How could they not be? They're staying at the mansion on the hill!"

"Yeah, you're right," I said, and I let the subject drop again. "I better start dipping the strawberries."

***

I placed perfectly arranged plates of Godiva chocolates, delicate French vanilla and lemon petits fours covered with icing in intricate floral and lattice designs, heart-shaped cucumber slices topped with mozzarella cheese and half a grape tomato drizzled with olive oil, and a crystal bowl of large chocolate dipped strawberries onto a glass and brass rolling tea cart dressed with white lace tablecloths. I nestled the chilled champagne, which Mary chose, in a brass, top hat bucket filled to the brim with ice and set it on the bottom shelf with two crystal goblets. The finishing touch was two crisp linen napkins folded into a heart-shape, with a fortune cookie wrapped with a red satin ribbon tied with a bow, tucked into each one. With that set up, I went out to the balcony to examine the over-stuffed cushions on the white wicker settee, looking for any signs of dust. Assured that they were spotless, I fluffed the yellow pillows at each end. I went inside, across the room to the open doorway, turned and took one last look around the room. Satisfied that everything was perfect, I closed the door.

I had just made it down to the kitchen, when they returned. I heard Mary's laughter in response to something Nick had said as they walked through the foyer and up the stairs to their room. I smiled to myself, *at least I know he has a sense of humor*. Then, I set the table for breakfast, sliced and arranged the fruit plate, programmed the coffee pot for 9:00 and went up to bed, praying I would get a good night's sleep.

***

Grace sat drinking a cup of coffee when I walked into the kitchen. "They'll be down for breakfast around 9:30," I told her.

"Yes, and everything will be ready. Your fruit plate is a work of art," she said as she slid it out of the refrigerator and set it onto a tray. I had carefully arranged stacks of peeled orange, kiwi, and strawberry slices around the plate with a whole strawberry, green leaf top attached, cut to fan out, in the center.

"I hope our guests approve," I said.

"Here they come," Grace said when we heard them on the stairs.

"Ok, here it goes." I picked up the tray and walked through the butler's pantry to the dining room.

Mary sat on the window seat looking out. "We

were just admiring your beautiful roses. What kind are they?"

"The pink, red, and yellow roses are American beauty, and the white ones are Iceberg."

"They're stunning," said Mary. Nick stood behind her with his hands in the pockets of his khakis, still no comment, but at least he was smiling.

I set the tray on the sideboard and carried the plate of fruit and a crystal pitcher of orange juice to the center of their table; then, I set a plate of fresh baked chocolate chip muffins on the side, along with a white thermal butler of hot coffee.

"Oh, how lovely," Mary exclaimed as she sat on the upholstered, blue taffeta chair. Nick joined her sitting in the matching chair across from her.

"Grace is preparing rosemary, artichoke with cheese omelets, crisp bacon and buttered whole wheat toast. I'll bring that in as soon as it's ready. Enjoy."

"Thank you," Nick said, preoccupied with pouring Mary's orange juice and then his own.

"You're welcome," I said and left the room, feeling like I had just been dismissed. "I think he can't wait to get this over with." I told Grace when I walked back into the kitchen. She had just slid the cooked, heart-shaped eggs onto warm china plates.

"I'm sure you're overreacting. Where's your confidence, girl," she teased. She added the bacon and a plate of toast to the tray. "Stop worrying and serve the eggs." With that she turned away from me and started washing dishes. I was being dismissed again, I couldn't believe it!

I went back to the dining room with the tray of food. I cleared their empty fruit plates and set the eggs, bacon and toast in front of them. “Oh, the eggs are hearts, how thoughtful,” Mary gushed.

“Yes, thank you,” Nick added.

I smiled and said, “You’re welcome,” turned and walked back out to the kitchen, quietly letting out a long, slow breath of relief that my time of seeing to their comfort and enjoyment was over. Grace and I had just finished cleaning up when we heard them go upstairs.

“They’ll be checking out soon,” I said with relief. “After they leave, I’m taking a nap. I’m drained.”

“Yeah, from the stress you put on yourself,” Grace said.

“Well, I can’t help it. I want them to have wonderful memories of their stay here on their anniversary”.

About thirty minutes later, we heard them. I went out to the foyer to see them off. Nick was carrying their overnight bag.

“We had a wonderful time,” Mary said. “I’m glad we decided to celebrate our anniversary here. We felt welcomed and pampered—like royalty.”

I hadn’t noticed that Nick had put the bag down. He gently took my hand in his, covered it with his other hand, smiled, and said, “Yes, everything was perfect.”

Guest Book Comments

“We’ll always remember our wonderful stay at Sunbrook on our tenth anniversary!”

Chapter 4

Mike moved in that night. My heart skipped a beat at the familiar rumble of his truck coming up the driveway. I met him at the door with a peck on the cheek. "Welcome home, Darling. Follow me."

I walked sideways up the stairs in front of him trying, but failing, to contain my excitement, resisting the urge to pull him up faster by the arm like an eager lover on a rendezvous. "I think you're going to like what I did with our room."

"If you say so," he said, trudging up each step like he was lifting lead boots. His shoulders hunched forward as if the small duffle bag he carried contained an extra pair. I felt a twinge of annoyance but pushed it aside, refusing to let his indifference dampen my enthusiasm. I stood at the top, waited until he reached my side, and then opened the door. With an outstretched arm, my hand swept across in a bold gesture presenting the room.

His sea-blue eyes widened. "You're right, I like it very much." The tiredness in his voice melted away with each word.

Fireplace flames cast a romantic glow as their shadows danced among the soft, yellow roses of the vintage wallpaper. The champagne, satin comforter with matching shams resting on two sets of plump pillows shimmered on the polished brass bed. The dreamy vignette enhanced the plush, scarlet and royal blue Oriental rug beneath it.

"Oh, I'm so glad," I said and slid my arms around his waist, laying my head against his chest. "I think it's perfect, and we are going to be happy in our amazing new home."

"Yes, very happy," he whispered into my hair. We held one another for a moment before he kissed the top of my head and released me. "I'm ready for a shower."

I opened the walk-in closet door, "Look, I arranged all your clothes on this side." I pointed to the wooden rack and shelves on the right. "Everything is at your fingertips. Here are your pajamas." I picked them up and held them out, but instead of taking them he pulled me close and planted a firm kiss on my lips, released me, then turned, and sauntered to the bathroom.

"I don't think we'll need pajamas tonight," he teased, as he disappeared through the door.

The sound of water pounding the porcelain tub, then, the forceful spray of the shower broke my surprise and wonder. I looked down. His pajamas had slipped from my palms and lay at my feet. I pulled my hands to my chest and lifted my shoulders to my ears, while my heart did a junior high skip. I relished in his display of attention and the thought that we would be alone in our room for the rest of the night. Then, fearing that someone or something would interfere with our interlude of love, I rushed out of the closet to the bedroom door, pushed it shut and locked out the complexities of life. My body relaxed now that I knew we were secure. I turned around facing the room and leaned against the door, relieved to hear the shower still running.

My eyes were drawn to the vanity laden with crystal perfume bottles, vintage atomizers sporting plump blue and lavender bulbs with tassels, along with delicate china jars filled with emollient creams and lotions to pamper every inch of a woman. I sat in front of the large round mirror to refresh my makeup. I applied more pink passion lip stain and then dotted a touch of gloss below my cupid's bow and the center of my lower lip. I removed my scarlet chiffon robe, letting it fall across the back of the chair and drape to the floor. I tousled my long dark curls with my fingers until they fell softly around my bare shoulders. I picked up a bottle of Chanel No. 5, Mike's favorite, and spritzed a touch onto my hair, neck, and inside my wrists and inner thighs. Then, stood up, turned back and forth in front of the mirror making sure that the black lace teddy revealed my body in all the right places. Satisfied with my results, I paused, smiled at my reflection, and whispered, "Tiffany, you know how to make a man feel welcome."

***

I awoke the next morning to sunlight streaming through the tall bedroom windows. The feel of Mike pressed against my bare back with his arm around my waist thrilled my heart. Our bodies felt as one. His soft snore at the back of my head tickled my neck as single strands of my hair bounced with each breath. It felt good to have his body close to mine, even after twenty years of marriage. We haven't grown tired of each other like some married couples. I closed my eyes and petitioned a silent prayer that we would always want and need each other. I became so overwhelmed with love that I pulled his hand up to my breast and snuggled closer.

"Good morning," he murmured into my hair and cupped my breast.

"Good morning," I replied and turned to face him. "We only have a few more minutes before we have to shower."

"Ok then! Let's make the most of it.

***

We went down to the kitchen where Mike cooked his usual Sunday breakfast of sausage, eggs, toast, and home fries. It wasn't long before Grace joined us and Mike fried up his delicious menu for her. "You're a good cook," she said after sampling the assortment on her plate.

"Thanks, but the only meal I can make is breakfast."

"Well, you're in the right place then," she said with a wry grin.

"Yeah, I guess so," he said smiling, amused by her comment.

"David told me he would be here this morning to help rake up the ocean of leaves behind the house. He also said he would take a look at the antique swing to see how much wood he'll need to repair it," I said. My Brother David had mastered the art of working with wood. His hand-built farm cupboards and benches were desired by many in Hollidaysburg and the surrounding counties.

"Good," Mike said. "We should be done cleaning the front porches before he arrives, and then we can rake all the leaves. We'll accomplish more that way. Besides, I need to take some time to check out the garage. I wanted to bring the Chevelle and the '39 Chevy here as soon as possible. They have been taking up room in Dad's garage far too long. He needs the space for his trucks."

The six-car garage intrigued Mike the most at Sunbrook. His cars were his passion. He loved everything about them: restoring them, working on them, cleaning them, and driving them. I think he would have had fifty cars if he had a place to store them. Sometimes, sounding like a spoiled child, I would confront him saying, "You like your cars more than you like me." Deep down I knew it wasn't true but couldn't help feeling that way. He had told me early in our marriage that he would not sit around with me after work six days a week. We spent Sundays together, that was it! I fought with him the first five years of our marriage until he told me he wasn't going to change. I gave in and filled the time with my own interests like photography and interior decorating. I even partnered with my mother and sister-in-law Gwen to open a successful consignment shop in downtown Hollidaysburg called 2nd Hand Rose. I got used to his way of thinking after a while, although I had felt slighted, like he didn't love me as much as I loved him. Now, with two businesses, I'm glad for my independence. Mike makes no demands on me like my friends' husbands do, such as have supper on the table every night.

We filled the day with a frenzy of work, slept sound, and Mike left for work early Monday morning. I worked on writing up the ad for the *Altoona Mirror* that "Sunbrook Mansion Bed and Breakfast is accepting reservations for weddings and parties. Book your Christmas Party now in the Victorian setting of a bygone era." I also had the master copies of the brochures and business cards, written in floral prose touting, "Enjoy an exquisite experience during your stay at Sunbrook Mansion Bed and Breakfast."

"I'm dropping off the brochures at the printers to be copied on my way to work. Will you pick them up before they close at four o'clock, Grace?"

"Sure, no problem," she said.

"Thanks, I'm leaving now. I'll see you later."

Gwen and I had worked late pricing ten racks of consignors' clothing. I stopped at the market on the way home and bought a chocolate comfort pie. Then, I walked through the kitchen door at seven o'clock, pleased to see the finished brochures on the table. I opened and arranged them on a cherry credenza inside the foyer door, along with a brass lamp topped with a fringed, cream, brocade shade, the guest book, and a red feather pen.

I walked to the bottom of the steps and yelled, "Grace, come down and join me for some hot tea and pie."

"Pie," she said, leaning over the balcony far above me. "I'll be right down."

I had water on to boil for tea and the pie sliced and on plates when she bounded through the doorway. "Mm, chocolate," she took the plate I held out without pausing and plopped down at the table.

I poured our tea, trayed it along with my pie, and joined her. She took a bite and with her mouth full mumbled, "It's good."

"What a treat, right?"

"Yeah, we deserve it. We made this place beautiful."

"Yes, it's hard to believe I'm here. I dreamed of this for so long. I'm so blessed."

"Yes, you are. You have a lot to be thankful for, but you worked hard for it," Grace said.

"I have labored, along with many wonderful friends and family. You've worked hard, too, since you've been here, Grace."

"Well, I've enjoyed it and look forward to working with you for a long time," she said.

"I'm glad. We make a good team."

"Yeah, we do."

We grew quiet and since neither of us was the warm fuzzy, huggy type, I stood up. "I'm going to bed. Tomorrow's guests are scheduled to check in around twelve." I reached down to fill the tray with our used china, but Grace flipped her hand back and forth over the tray.

"Go on to bed. I'll clean up here. Good night."

"Good night, Grace," I walked across the kitchen, feeling the smooth Georgia pine under my bare feet. I started up the stairs, holding onto the railing, and felt a gentle touch on my hand. I paused, looked down at my gold bracelet, an anniversary gift from Mike, and thought that it must have brushed my hand. Then, I continued up the stairs with a prayer of "*Thanks for*

Grace" on my lips.

Guest Book Comments

"We have loved every minute of our stay in your beautiful home."

Chapter 5

On my way downstairs in the morning, I heard an oldies song playing from the radio in the kitchen.

"Good morning," Grace said with a bright smile when I entered. "Shake, rattle and roll," she sang, a little off key, shaking her butt in time with the music as she stacked cups in the cupboard.

I giggled. "It is a good morning. Our guests are arriving around noon. They're staying in the *Bridal Chamber*. I checked it before I came down, and it's perfect, so all we have to do is relax and wait. I haven't read a book in months, so I'm going to take my breakfast into the music room, prop up my feet, and get lost in the romance novel I bought at the market yesterday."

"Ok, don't get up if the phone rings. I'll answer it."

"You're a gem, Grace," I walked through the foyer and into the music room. My heels clicked against the oak, parquet floor as I crossed to the rose, wing chair in the far corner. I placed the tray on the mahogany end table and sat, my body sinking into the plush velvet. I flipped off my shoes and rested my feet on the matching tuffet.

I looked up at the ornate, plaster ceiling. Gold leaf accented the crafted curly cues that soldiered around the edge and on the center medallion above a large, crystal chandelier. The morning sun saturated each crystal with rainbows of color, dazzling my senses. My collection of enamel music boxes decorated the fireplace mantle and various accent tables about the room. Antique pictures with a musical theme and gold sconces graced the soft yellow walls.

I ate my toast and sipped my tea, then picked up the novel, and began to read. I had just turned the page to the second chapter, when my favorite music box started playing. My eyes darted around the room, spotting no one, but it felt as if someone had joined me. Surprised that I wasn't afraid and couldn't explain its spectral beginning, I leaned my head back and closed my eyes. The *Titanic* tune filled the room, '*You're here, there's nothing I fear and I know that my heart will go on.*' I listened, enjoying each twinkling note, enchanted by the magic of Sunbrook Mansion.

***

The music box had silenced and I had a quarter of my novel read, when the doorbell rang. I jumped up, took my cup to the kitchen and hastened to the door. I opened it to an attractive young couple. "Welcome, I'm Tiffany. Please, come in." They stepped through the door, their luggage trailing them.

"Hi, I'm Ben, and this is my wife, Laura."

"It's wonderful to have you at Sunbrook," I said, a bit on the excited side.

"Well, I'm happy to be here, this is beautiful and so charming," Laura said as we walked further into the foyer.

"Follow me, I'll show you where I'll be serving

the morning meal. This is the library, and through here is the dining room. What time would you like breakfast?"

"I love this. I'm so looking forward to eating in here," Laura said and then turned to Ben, "What time, honey?"

"How about eight-thirty? I would like to sleep in for a change. I host an early morning radio show, so I have to be up at four-thirty, five days a week." Laura nodded in agreement.

"Then, eight-thirty it is. I'll show you to your room, now." We walked back to the stairs, where they grabbed their luggage and followed. "This is actually the Bridal Chamber. I thought you might enjoy the romantic décor." I opened the door and stepped aside as they trailed thru.

"Yes, how thoughtful of you," Laura said. She left her suitcase by the bed and disappeared into the bathroom, where we heard her squeal, "Oh, I love the old fashioned tub and pedestal sink!"

"I think this is perfect," Ben said.

"I had just opened for business last month, and would appreciate feedback on your stay. Good or bad, we want to hear about it. Let me or my assistant Grace know if you need anything. And if it's during the night, I'm in the room at the top of the stairs. Just knock."

"Ok, thank you," Ben said as I stepped out of the room.

I went back downstairs and made another cup of tea before going back to the music room. Between reading and sitting down to lunch and supper, I had all the guests checked into their rooms by six o'clock: Ron, an airline pilot, here on a layover in the Trust room; George and Sharon, a middle-aged couple from Virginia in the Deborah; and Sam from Ohio in the Carrie Ann.

When Mike arrived home from work, I was in bed and struggling to stay awake while watching TV. "Hi hon, all the guests are here and settled in," I turned off the television. "I'm going to sleep. I have to get up at six-thirty. Go ahead and take a shower, you won't disturb me. Just give me a goodnight kiss before you go in."

"Gladly," he crossed the room and gave me a peck on the lips. "That's the best I can do for now. I've been greasing the underneath of trucks all day, and I'm covered in it. So you don't want me to touch you."

"You know I always welcome your touch, but I'll comply this time," I teased. He walked into the bathroom. I yawned and snuggled down into the comforter. "By the way," I mumbled, drifting off, "We have a ghost."

Guest Book Comments

"Your treasures are wonderful–the pancakes and breakfast were super delicious, too!"

Chapter 6

I woke up before the alarm rang, dressed, applied my makeup, and pulled my hair up into a neat bun. Checked myself in the mirror to make sure that I looked presentable for serving breakfast and then went downstairs to find Grace in the kitchen making coffee.

"Good morning, Grace. I'll get the fruit plate ready if you'll make the mini muffins."

"Sounds good to me." She read the recipe and then poured the flour into the measuring cup. "Did you sleep well or were you too excited about this morning?"

"My nerves were a little on edge until I took a warm bath which relaxed me. So, I didn't have any trouble sleeping. I feel good about having a full house. We are well prepared, and I don't think we overlooked anything. Although, there could be some surprises. We'll know soon enough when the guests come down. But I'm relaxed for now."

I had just put the fruit plate in the refrigerator when Mike walked in and helped himself to a cup of coffee. "Do you want some sausage and eggs?" I asked.

"No, I'll just pour myself a bowl of cereal. You can make me some toast if you want to, though."

"Ok." I made his toast and sat at the table to

chat while he ate. I didn't bring up the mysterious painting noises and the unwound music box. I knew he didn't hear me tell him about a ghost last night because he didn't wake me and press the issue. The thought of his reaction filled me with apprehension, but I decided to tell him again tonight.

***

Mike picked up his coat and turned to me, "Well, I'm going to take off. I have to stop at *Allegheny Trucks* for parts on the way to work. Dad and I are greasing another truck today so I'll have more clothes that will need to soak in degreaser before they're washed."

"No problem! I'll wait until you're done and do yesterday's and today's together." Then, I leaned close and whispered, "Or Grace will."

"I heard that." I turned around to see her glaring at me over the top of her reading glasses, today's paper lay in front of her on the table.

"No, I guess I will." I said. Mike and I put our heads close together and snickered.

"Leave a bucket ready by the washer tonight, and I'll take my clothes off down here and put them in to soak."

"Good plan," Grace said, not lifting her eyes from the paper.

I nodded in agreement while holding back another snicker.

"See you tonight," Mike said, gave me a quick kiss and a wink, and then walked out to his pickup.

I stood in the doorway and watched him slide onto the seat and start his truck. He put his arm part way out the window and waved as he pulled out of the drive way.

I went back inside just in time to hear the guests coming down for breakfast. I filled the tray with fruit, muffins and coffee and carried it into the dining room, looking forward to another day at Sunbrook Mansion.

After breakfast, the guests started to depart for their antique shopping, visits with relatives, and sightseeing. I caught Ben and Laura in the foyer on their way out. "Going out? I'll freshen up your room before you return."

"We won't be back until late this evening. We're spending the day with my parents, and they won't want us to leave. They have our whole day planned," Ben said.

"I wanted to ask you, how is your stay? Is your room ok?"

"The room is lovely, but hot," Laura said. "We slept well after we opened the window to let in some cool air."

"Oh, I'm so sorry. The temperature dropped into the thirties, so I turned up the thermostat. I didn't realize the radiator worked so well in that room. I guess I'll have separate thermostats installed in each room so that guests can regulate the temperature to their liking."

"No apologies necessary. We were fine. Laura lingered in the bath this morning. At home, she has to get in, wash and get out before the water gets too cold."

"Yes, a bath is a treat for me. It was nice to relax

and enjoy it."

"We just wanted to inform you about the heat for the benefit of your future guests," Ben said.

"Thank you, on behalf of my future guests."

"We better get going; my parents will be upset with us if we're late." They both looked at each other in mutual agreement, as couples do.

"Well, you have a nice time, and I'll see you tomorrow at breakfast."

With all the guests out for the day, I went upstairs to refresh their rooms. I made the beds and wiped around the sink and tub. Then, I bundled up the soiled towels and replaced them with clean ones. When I finished and double checked that nothing was overlooked, I went down to help Grace clean the dining room and kitchen. I answered several calls from people inquiring about holiday parties and set up appointments for next week. Grace had left to visit her mother, so I hung out, manning the phone. I also called the service department of a furnace company to get an estimate for installing the thermostats. It's probably going to be high, but it will be worth dipping into the savings to make sure my guests are comfortable.

I relished my time alone with Sunbrook and wandered from room to room. The library with its dark paneled walls wasn't as bright as its adjoining rooms. The large floor-to-ceiling fireplace and the bookshelves along the walls absorbed some of its light. The old pines and full maple trees planted during Sunbrook's youth towered outside the windows. They filtered the sunlight across the floor resulting in silhouettes of limbs grasping on to their leaves that fluttered in the breeze. I took off my shoes to feel the warmth of the oak floor beneath my feet. The shadows climbed past my toes and up my legs as I walked within their reach. I lifted my skirt to expose my pale thighs, darkening them with nature's artwork. I peered down at the view and wished for a phantom photographer to take a photo of this heavenly canvas that would disappear as the sun moved on. I blushed at the thought of it and viewed the snapshot until it faded. I walked to a chair by the window, picked up my romance novel from the marble top end table, and began to read.

Guest Book Comments

"Sunbrook is beautiful. Thank you so much for making us feel so welcomed."

Chapter 7

I had just finished reading my book when I noticed the sun shining from the west. Its circle of sienna hung low in the sky, announcing suppertime. My stomach growled in agreement. I walked to the kitchen and retrieved from the refrigerator a container of Mulligan stew left over from last night's supper. Grace had made it from a recipe she said, "Looked so scrumptious and, best of all, easy," that she tore from a tattered woman's magazine she leafed through while waiting for her mother at the doctor's office. I spooned the beef stew into the pan and turned the burner on high. My hunger and impatience rose with the heat as if willing the "scrumptious" brew to boil. I poured myself a glass of milk and buttered a slice of bread, while listening for the bubbling. It wasn't long before my piping hot meal was ready. My stomach growled again prompting me to fill it. I ladled the stew into a bowl and placed it on a tray, added the milk and bread, lifted the tray, and hurried up the stairs. I stopped at the top, bewildered. The mannequin, dressed in the designer wedding gown, for brides to rent, had been moved. It normally overlooked the staircase. Now, it stood across the vestibule in front of my collection of vintage purses I had arranged on the wall. I set the tray on a small table by my bedroom door and walked over to inspect it. The cumbersome and heavy gown wasn't easy to move. "Now how did you get over here?" I asked out loud. Then, it dawned on me that Grace might have moved it to polish the railing and spindles it was blocking. I dismissed any suspicion and grabbed my still steaming supper from the table.

I settled on the bed, with the tray on my lap, picked up the remote and pressed. Menacing music filled the room as opening credits burst onto the screen. I ate while watching the FBI's BAU team profile and apprehend a vicious serial killer. I heard the random return of my guests throughout the hour. It would be another hour before Mike would be home, so I showered, put on my nightgown, and got back into bed.

TV 10 News anchors introduced themselves on the screen as Mike crept backwards through the door wearing his long johns and socks. "I think I made it upstairs without anyone seeing me."

"Oh no, I didn't put your robe in the laundry room." My face flushed hot with shame at my thoughtlessness. I wanted to ease his mind of any embarrassment. "I'm sure no one saw you. All the guests are in their rooms for the night."

"Whatever." He walked into the bathroom without even a glance my way, showing me that he was upset by my oversight.

I sat up in bed when he came out from his shower. I was anxious to talk and make things right, but he got into bed turned his back to me, and muffled, "Good night" into his pillow, letting me know that he was still fuming and didn't want to talk. Mike's laid-back personality helped him refrain from anger in most situations, but the possibility of strangers catching him in such a state of undress would have been humiliating.

I made a mental note to hang his terry cloth robe by the washer first thing tomorrow. I almost put him in a compromising position and intended to make sure it wouldn't happen again. It would be futile to try to make up now. I knew Mike well, and he would not get over this tonight. But I loved him and had to let him know that I felt bad. I switched off the light, lay down and, knowing it would be met with silence, made my first attempt to heal the hurt, and offered a heartfelt, "I'm sorry."

I lay in the darkness chastising myself while my mind juggled the day's events. In an effort to dismiss those thoughts, I reviewed the next day's schedule. The early start and full day required a good night's sleep. I closed my eyes, took a deep yoga breath in, held it for a few seconds, then exhaled long and slow, willing my body to relax. Then, my eyes flew open. A quick, shallow breath and tightened muscles awakened my nerves, flinging them to the edge. My mind had betrayed me by remembering that I still hadn't told Mike about the strange occurrences. I breathed out in frustration. I needed to move. I swung my leg out over the side of the bed intending to rise, but hesitated when a sweet fragrance of jasmine filled the room. I inhaled the flowery scent, filling my senses and sending me into a garden of bliss. I pulled my leg back under the covers as the tension departed, coaxing my nerves from the edge and lulling them back to calm. I closed my eyes and smiled in the darkness at the feeling of the gentle brush of fingers across my cheek. Then, drifted off to sleep.

Guest Book Comments

"Thanks so much for making us feel at home–like part of the family–we love Sunbrook!"

Chapter 8

When I awoke, the sun had already lifted the morning mist. The beams of light reached down through the tall windows revealing tiny dust motes dancing as if they were happy to be found. I took a moment to enjoy their graceful ballet within Sunbrook's stately architecture of wide, white moldings and paneled wooden doors. The ruffled, vintage sheer curtains framing the windows filtered some of the sunlight, reminiscent of the background in a dream. I sighed when I turned and found the space empty beside me. Mike had left without waking me with my morning kiss. I got up, walked straight to the closet, pulled out his terry bathrobe and hung it over the hook on the bedroom door so I wouldn't forget it on my way out. I went back into the closet and chose a pink cotton dress and matching flats. I laid the dress on the bed and set the shoes on the floor below. My bedside clock startled me with its loud monotonous buzz, announcing that I had to be downstairs in twenty minutes to serve breakfast. I rushed to the bathroom, washed my face and brushed my teeth. I returned, pulled the dress down over my head, slipped on my shoes, sat at the vanity, and hurriedly put on my makeup. My bushy hair needed to be tamed, but there was no time for the curling iron, so I pinned it up into a loose bun. I examined my handiwork in the mirror. The concealer I patted over the dark circles under my eyes did a good job of hiding the evidence of only a few hours of sleep. My makeup proved flawless after I blended a spot of foundation over my brow. My hair frizzed out a bit, but it rendered a soft, romantic look. Satisfied with my efforts, my eyes were drawn past my reflection to focus on the empty bed, reinforcing my heavy heart. The thought of acting cheerful while serving my guests their breakfast brought me to despair. I leaned forward, bowing my head in defeat, and rested my elbows on the vanity, resisting the urge to cover my face with my hands and cry. Then a wisp of jasmine swirled around me. I felt a slight pressure on my shoulder as if someone had laid a hand there to comfort me. I flipped my head up to look in the mirror, but no one stood behind me. I inhaled the sweet fragrance, lifting my shoulders to take it all in. My body unfurled like a flower in spring reaching for the sun's warmth, chasing away my sorrow. I stood up, straightened my back, and lifted my chin. I had a job to do and the guests wouldn't wait. I walked out of the room and down the stairs with Mike's robe resting over my arm.

I entered the kitchen, "Good morning, Grace." She stood at the stove twirling a spatula like a baton, watching a skillet of green peppers and onions hiss and crackle in a pool of hot bacon grease.

"Mornin'," she said, not looking my way, her wide eyes glued to the skillet as if in a trance.

I kept walking to the laundry room where I hung the robe on a rack beside the washer. I walked back to the kitchen and noticed plates piled high with bacon and buttered toast sitting under the warming light. The full coffee pot sat steaming, ready to be poured into the thermal butlers.

"I see you have everything under control."

"Not the fruit, that's your forté"

I pulled from the refrigerator two large plates filled with a kaleidoscope of assorted of berries, oranges, and kiwi that I had cut and arranged last night. I filled the butlers with coffee, placed it all on a tray and carried it into the dining room. I set the coffee at each end of the table along with cream and sugar and two frosty pitchers of orange juice. I had just finished up when I heard the guests coming down the stairs. I grabbed the empty tray and rushed back to the kitchen where Grace had two baskets of fresh baked cinnamon muffins ready for me to add to the table. Without hesitation, I plucked them up and scrambled back to the dining room. I dropped them in their allotted space and exited through the pantry door as the first guest appeared around the corner from the foyer.

"Whew, I escaped just in time."

"What do you care if they see you setting the table? Afraid they'll find a fork cock-eyed and say to your face, 'How dare you? Straighten that fork now!'" She stood there smiling, looking pleased with her taunt, waiting for my reaction.

"Stop teasing, Grace," I feigned stomping my foot and returned the smile. "I wanted them to ease into their morning with good coffee and fellowship before I greeted them and served their breakfast.

Besides, I thought it would be nice for them to walk in and see a beautiful table laden with all their needs to start the day. You know, to feel pampered like at a first rate hotel."

"First off, they're not paying The Ritz rates and you already do more than enough to make them feel pampered. Look at the variety, not to mention the size of this breakfast." She fanned her hand out over the ample platters.

"Ok, Grace, could you just humor me for now?" I looked at the clock. "It's time for me to serve this horn-of-plenty." I gave her a side glance with a smile and I started filling the tray with the platters of bacon and the toast. She layered the last omelet onto an oval platter and dropped the platter onto the tray. "Grace!"

"Oh, sorry! I don't want to startle the eggs—they might lose their fluff and the guests won't feel pampered." She said, mimicking my side glance and smile.

I shook my head, turned, and, with the tray-of-abundance in my arms, sashayed out of the kitchen.

The dining room sang with a chorus of conversation and laughter. The week had ended and they were enjoying their last breakfast together. I couldn't help thinking that with each morning I observed their change from tentative, to friendly, and now to downright jovial.

"Good morning, everyone, I hope you slept well," I said, setting my tray onto the buffet.

"Good morning, Tiffany," they all bellowed. "Of course, we did...like a log....sweetest dreams," they chimed in nodding to each other in agreement.

"Wonderful! I'm pleased to hear it." I set the platters in front of them. "Today we're serving bacon and omelets filled with mild goat cheese, sundried tomatoes, green peppers, and onions. And, of course, plenty of buttered sourdough toast."

"What a perfect ending to a superb week at Sunbrook," Sam said, rubbing his palms together. The other guests concurred in unison. He picked up the tongs and lifted several slices of bacon onto his plate before passing it on. Then, he chose an omelet from the next platter passed his way.

I looked on with pleasure at their hearty appetites and their enjoyment of Sunbrook's hospitality. After all, like I keep telling Grace, that is what Sunbrook is all about.

Guest Book Comments

"Had a relaxing stay, and breakfast was delicious."

Chapter 9

I stood in the open doorway and waved goodbye to Ben and Laura, the last guests to check out, waiting until their car disappeared down the driveway before closing the door and going back to the kitchen. My ears flinched at the disturbing rattle of china that came from the dining room as Grace cleared the table. I started in to help her, not getting very far before she walked in with the large tray of dirty dishes. She set it on the counter then began loading the cups and saucer into the dishwasher.

"I'll get the rest of the dishes," I said, picking up an empty tray.

"No need, this is the last of them."

"Oh, ok." I put the tray away, walked over to the sink, and lowered the crystal pitchers and bowls into the soapy water with care. "Ben and Laura said the bridal chamber was too warm the first night. I turned up the thermostat because the temperature outside dipped below freezing. Would you mind if we took turns sleeping in each room for a couple of nights? It's important to make sure they are comfortable for the guests."

"That sounds like fun, sleeping in a different room every night. I'll feel like I'm a world traveler." She raised one shoulder, lifted her chin toward it, showing me a haughty profile and added, "Daarling."

Her performance made me laugh. "Hey, the wedding gown standing near the stairs, did you move it in front of the vintage purse wall?"

"No, but I did notice its new place and thought to myself, 'There she goes again, changing things around because she second guesses every detail'."

I ignored her snide comment, grinned, and forgave her for it. "Well, I'll move it back and hope it stays put this time."

"Let me know if you need any help. I put the table linens in the washer. They should be about done, so I might as well go check on them." She turned and disappeared into the laundry room.

I hustled upstairs to strip the beds. More guests were arriving tomorrow, so the sheets had to be changed right away. I reached the top and did a double take, then backed up to the antique settee, sat, and studied the wedding gown, which now stood in its original spot by the railing. My mind searched for an answer to the puzzle. I shook my head to clear it and chuckled at myself. "This dress wasn't going to sprout legs and walk. Perhaps one of the guests moved it over and then back as a prank." Satisfied with the solution, I headed to the Deborah room but gave one last glance over my shoulder. Something about the gown getting moved nagged at me, but I couldn't identify it.

I had finished taking all the linens off the beds and chucked them over the banister, just missing Grace.

"Hey! Watch it, up there! There's a person trying

to work down here, ya know?"

I ran down the steps, kicked the sheets into a tight pile, and scooped up as much as my arms could hold. "That's what you get for making fun of me earlier," I teased.

Grace stopped dusting, picked up the rest of the sheets, and followed me into the laundry room. I dropped my bundle on the floor, and Grace added hers.

"Thanks, Grace."

"You're welcome," she said and left to finish dusting. I opened the washer lid and started streaming the sheets in as one long continuous line until filling the tub to capacity. Then, I added detergent and bleach and pushed the buttons for hot water and extra-large load. I went to the sink for a drink of water and heard Grace talking, "Where's my dust cloth? I laid it on the hall table."

I walked out to the foyer to see her down on all fours with her head and shoulders under the table. She backed out empty handed and rose to her feet. "I don't see it anywhere. I could swear...," her voice faded. She stood with her hands on her hips. Furrowing her brow, her eyes darted back and forth, like she was retracing her steps in her mind.

"I'll get you another one, Grace." I pulled out a cloth from under the sink and tossed it her way. She caught it and gave me a thumbs up. "I'm sure we'll come across it. Maybe even in the laundry with the sheets." The telephone rang. I went into my office to answer it.

I returned to find that Grace had resumed dusting.

"Grace, that was Gwen on the phone. I'm going to change clothes and meet her at 2nd Hand Rose to price clothes. We have several full racks, so I'll be gone for a few hours. Call me if you need anything."

"Ok, I'll finish up the laundry in between dusting and then make the beds. But I'll let the towels for you since you're so fussy about how they're folded."

"Great," I said and then leapt up the stairs two at a time to change.

***

I pulled into the garage after work, tired but feeling good about how much Gwen and I had accomplished. We priced and hung all the clothes consigners had dropped off last week. 2nd Hand Rose was a popular resale store, so we over-booked our consignment appointments. It could be tough to stay caught up every week. Because of Gwen's outgoing and friendly personality, we had a loyal clientele. She took the time to make everyone who walked through the door feel welcome and important.

I opened the car door and held on to use it to pull myself up out of the seat. The muscles in my legs and back were sore from standing too long and had stiffened up on the drive home. I shut the door and walked toward the kitchen, but a show-stopping scene through the garage window caught my attention. Despite my pain, I stepped outside, looked toward the sky, stretched out my arms, and twirled under a golden shower of ginkgo leaves that rained from the large canopy of a stately tree along the driveway. A gentle breeze shook them loose and sent them down, glistening in the sunlight like tiny rice-paper fans. Thousands of them fluttered back and forth trying to catch an upward current to prolong their glorious air show then made a slow decent to the pavement, layering themselves into a carpet of gold. A gray cloud broke the spell. It floated in front of the sun, closing out the light like a dark, heavy stage curtain. A gust of wind blew the leaves up around me. I covered my eyes against the cyclone of fine dust they brought with them, then felt rain drops, and ran inside to the kitchen window. The rain pounded down in torrents, soaking the delicate leaves and washing them in temporary streams down the driveway and over the bank. The enchantment of Sunbrook filled me, and I offered a silent prayer of thanks for its unexpected moment of magic. In response, a wave of warmth enveloped me, as if being hugged.

Guest Book Comments

"Our room was wonderful. We enjoyed the peace and quiet."

Chapter 10

"Hi Tiffany, what are you looking at?" Grace walked through the kitchen and stood beside me. She leaned forward with her hands on the window sill and looked up and down the driveway. "I don't see anything."

The rain had slowed to a gentle shower. I stood silent, enjoying its tranquil tapping on the breakfast nook roof above us for a few seconds more before I answered her. "It's beautiful, the tree is beautiful."

"What tree?" She turned back to the window and peered up and down the driveway again, not seeing the tree right in front of her. She gave up and looked me up and down. "You're wet and you have leaves in your hair. How did you get caught in the rain when you parked in the garage?"

Still deriving pleasure from golden leaves and tempestuous weather, I ignored her question. "Listen to the soothing sound of the rain on the roof." I looked at her while I still focused on hearing every drop.

She shivered, pulled the sweater she wore closer to her neck with one hand, and hugged her middle with the other. "What are you talking about? The rain is dreary, and it's cold in here. I'm building a fire." She left the kitchen in a huff, pulling me from my reverie.

I walked over to check my hair in the mirror. A

couple of ginkgo leaves protruded from my tangled mass of dark curls. I coaxed each one out and tucked them between the pages of the cookbook beside me on the counter. At my first opportunity, I'd mount them in a scrapbook as a memento of my whimsical whirl with Sunbrook.

I pulled a bottle of rosé from the wine cooler, grabbed two glasses from the cupboard, and joined Grace in the library where she already had a blazing fire. "I brought wine," I sang.

She pushed my hand aside. "Are you kidding? I'm having a beer." She whooshed past me, headed for the kitchen. She came back with two bottles of beer. "This Bud's for you." She smiled as she held it out.

"Oh, why not," I set the wine and glasses on the table and took the Bud Lite. We sat in the matching velvet wing chairs in front of the fireplace and each took a swig.

"Aah, now this is livin'," Grace said, took another long swig, and then stared into the fire.

"I agree." We sat for a while and talked in front of the relaxing fire as we drank a couple of more beers. I looked up to view the flames' shadows frolicking on the walls around us. A movement on the staircase landing caught my attention. "I didn't hear Mike come home." I jumped up and yelled to our room, "I'll be up in a little while, Mike."

"Why wouldn't he stop in and talk to us before going up?" Grace asked.

I sighed. "Because he's upset with me, he had to come upstairs in his underwear last night. I forgot to leave his robe in the laundry room."

"So you forgot. Big deal! He'll get over it," she lifted her bottle in a toast.

"You're right! He'll get over it." I raised my bottle toward hers. We both laughed and drank up.

"My beer's empty." She stood up with her hand out to take my empty bottle. "Ready for another one?"

"No, I'm feeling tipsy from drinking on an empty stomach. I'm grabbing a snack and going up to bed." We swayed, arm in arm, out to the kitchen. I opened the refrigerator, decided to nix the snack, and grabbed a bottle of water instead. "Good night, Grace. We can sleep in tomorrow. The guests won't arrive until after five o'clock."

"Then, I'm having another beer and enjoying the fire until it goes out. Good night." She made her way back to the library with one hand sliding along the wall and a fresh beer dangling from the other hand. I followed her into the foyer and stopped at the bottom of the stairs.

The walls spun around me, so I held onto the railing before stepping up. I stood still with both feet flat on the first step to make sure I had my bearings before I lifted my foot to take another one. I imagined the peril of a long, hard fall backwards, so I kept climbing like that until reaching the top. Darkness met me when I opened the bedroom door. The hall light cast its glow across the empty bed, where I expected to see Mike lay sleeping. I made my way to the bathroom where nothing had been touched, a sign that Mike had never been there. "But I saw him on the landing. At least I think I did," I slurred to myself out loud. I had already drunk two beers and fatigue had caught up with me by the time I glimpsed the figure on the stairs, so maybe I was hallucinating.

I flipped on the bedroom light switch and maneuvered my way across the room where I set the water bottle on the bedside table. I turned toward the closet when my breath caught in my throat, and I stumbled backward onto the bed. Mike stood in the doorway.

"Mike! Why didn't you say something or at least make some noise? You almost scared me to death!"

"I didn't mean to. I took off my boots downstairs while I talked to Grace. She's wasted, and so are you. I watched you stumbling, and it smells like a brewery in here."

"Yeah, I'm listing a little. Hey, I saw you on the stairs an hour ago, why didn't you come into the library to join Grace and me then?"

"You didn't see me. I only got here a few minutes ago."

"Ooh." I gave up thinking about it and moaned as I flopped back on the bed. "Don't wake me. I'm sleeping in."

"I'm not surprised. I would bet, by the condition you're in, you probably won't be up before noon."

"Whatever," I mumbled. Then rolled onto my side and passed out.

When I opened my eyes, I still lay on my side. My arm tingled with needles, and my shoulder ached. I faced the bold stare of the clock on the table. Its black hands reaching up to emphasize noon like an explanation point. I slid my legs out over the side of the bed and sat up. I wavered back and forth, or the room did, I wasn't sure. I shook my arm and massaged its length until the needles subsided. I sat for a few minutes, then picked up the bottle of water from the table, twisted off the cap, and took a sip. My thirst raged, but I started with small sips until I felt sure my stomach would cooperate. I drank half the bottle before I stood up and walked without faltering into the bathroom to start my day with a shower.

Grace sat at the table in her pajamas drinking a cup of coffee when I walked into the kitchen. "How are you feeling, Grace? How long have you been up?"

"I got up around ten-thirty, came down and made the coffee, poured myself a cup, sat down, and haven't moved since."

Her pale complexion displayed a tint of green. I put my hand over my mouth trying to contain my laughter. She must have seen the humor in my eyes because she looked at me with disdain. The laughter I fought to hold at the back of my throat burst out. I couldn't stop, and it brought tears to my eyes. The thought of her sitting there all that time was so out of her character that the comedy of it had me in stitches. I struggled to get control and catch my breath then slowed down enough to draw a quick breath, but she rolled her eyes, and my laughter erupted again.

Her stern, hard stare went along with her serious tone when she commanded, "That's enough."

My laughter slowed and then stopped. Dismayed by her reaction, I froze a smile, hoping to lighten her mood. She didn't bulk, her expression stayed stern, so I started babbling. "Aw, come on, Grace, I didn't mean to be insensitive, but the fact that your hangover is so bad that you've been sitting here green to the gills since this morning is hilarious. You're always full of energy, bustling around getting things done."

My babbling stopped when she averted her eyes and turned her head to look out the window. The corners of her mouth turned up into a smile, "Well, alrighty then."

I realized by her sudden change in demeanor that she had pretended to be angry with me. So there was only one thing I had left to say, "Touché."

The telephone rang and I answered it. "Tonight's guests just canceled. They're sick with the flu."

Grace eased out of her chair, her hands flat on the table, pushing herself up until her knees locked. She stood for a few seconds and then hobbled toward the door. "Thank God. I'm going back to bed."

Guest Book Comments

"Thank you for our pleasant stay at your mountain mansion."

Chapter 11

A day off, I couldn't believe it—me time! It's been so long—choosing how to spend it eluded me. Not sure of my new-found freedom, I checked my desk calendar. I knew it was too good to be true—the heating technician would be here at three to survey the rooms and quote me an estimate for installing the thermostats. The clock on my desk showed only an hour to spare. Reading a book in the library would be the most enjoyable way to spend it. Part of the pleasure was finding the right one. I scanned the first shelf, sliding my fingers across the spines, reading the titles. The romance novels lined the top. The classics followed, not in the mood for nineteenth century literature. Next in line, biographies, perfect! I skimmed the titles until finding, *Survivors of the Titanic,* a recent addition to my collection. My fascination with the *Titanic* began in ninth grade history class. After that, I hungered for any information on the disaster. I read all the books in the local libraries then scoured flea markets, antique shops, and thrift stores for anything *Titanic.* I found books, puzzles, games, models, and even paintings of the ship. The whole collection, with Sunbrook's library as a back drop, transformed me back to 1912. I pulled the volume from the shelf and cradled it on my arm. Then, ran my fingers, with reverence, over the photo of the Titanic on the cover. I hugged the book close and picked up my glasses from the marble-topped table. I sat down, tucked my feet under me on the smooth leather of the over-stuffed chair, and opened to the first page.

The doorbell rang and I jumped, almost dropping my book. I half stood up and slipped it behind me on the chair, then gave it an I'll-be-back pat, and walked to the foyer. The technician had his face against the glass with both hands on each side to block the light while he peered through the door's window. He pulled back when I got closer, as if embarrassed to get caught. He stood aloof, looking at everything but the door, and then acted surprised when I opened it.

"Hello, please come in."

"Hi, I'm Jason. I'm here to quote an estimate for installing thermostats."

"Yes, I'm Tiffany. I'm the one who called. Follow me upstairs to the bedroom." I turned and walked toward the stairs but not before catching his hazel eyes widen for a second when I told him to follow me to the bedroom. He walked up the stairs behind me. I kept my face forward, hiding my smile, surprised at myself for not feeling any embarrassment for my risqué command. I led him into the bridal chamber to the radiator. "This one is much smaller than the radiators in the other rooms, but when I turned the thermostat up, the other rooms were comfortable while this one became as hot as a sauna. Follow me! I'll show you the other bedrooms." We walked from room to room until he knew exactly what I needed. We walked out into the vestibule.

"I've seen all I need to here. Now, I would like to see your boiler."

"Ok, we'll take the elevator to the basement."

"Elevator, you have an elevator?"

"Yes, and it's the only way to the basement from inside the house." His eyes widened in surprise when I opened what could be mistaken for a closet door. The automatic light filled a compartment large enough to carry three people. I pushed aside the brass accordion gate. "The *Titanic* had gates just like this in its elevators." I swept my hand toward the inside. "After you."

"Wh…wh…what? His chin dropped, and eyes were as round as plates. "Are you sure it's safe? It looks kind of rickety."

"Yes, it's safe. The inspector checked it last month. You aren't afraid, are you?"

"No!" He gave me a scowl and stepped inside.

I followed him in and pulled the door shut, slid the gate closed until it latched, then pressed the down button. The elevator jerked, and Jason slapped the palms of his hands against the sides to brace himself. The slow descent could be unnerving if you weren't used to it. Jason's breathing became quick and shallow. "This thing isn't going to trap us in here, is it?"

"No, and if we were trapped, there's a phone to call for help." I pointed to the black 1960's vintage wall phone.

"That thing's ancient… are you sure it works?"

"Of course it works. The inspector checked it, too?" We settled to an abrupt stop. Jason let out a small whimper. His wide eyes in his pale face stared at the accordion gate. He stood poised for an escape as soon as it opened. "It's ok, Jason. We're safe and in the basement." I slid the gate back and opened the door before he went into a panic. He leaped forward like a greyhound through the starting gate at a dog race. He didn't stop until he stood in the middle of the light-filled room, well clear of the elevator.

I stepped out and closed the elevator door to assure him that I wouldn't force him back in. "It's ok, Jason. We'll go out the cellar door after you're done here. The furnace is in the next room." I switched on the light. We entered the room and stopped in front of the furnace. He walked around it, bent down to read something on the side, and then wrote it down on his clipboard. He stood up and walked around to the other side, looked up at the pipes, then wrote more information down. "Ok, I'm done here. Which way is out?"

Taken aback by his abruptness, I asked, "That didn't take very long. Are you sure you got everything?"

"Yes, let's go." He looked around like he expected, at any minute, that someone would jump out at us. "This place gives me the creeps." He looked down at his arms then started rubbing one with his hand. "I got goosebumps. Come on, show me the way out."

A giggled interrupted our exchange. We jerked our heads and peered through the entrance into the darkness of the next room. I strained my ears listening for more laughter and then took a step toward the darkness. Jason retreated behind me. "Let's get the hell out of here."

I turned and saw Jason's pallor, his eyes wide with fear. "Ok, it's this way." I hurried toward the concrete steps and lead him out of the basement. He passed me and took off for his car before I cleared the top step. He had opened the door and slid onto the seat while I hurried to catch up with him. He scribbled some figures on his clipboard then jabbed a copy at me. "Here's the estimate. If you want our company to do the job, call and ask for Jim Burns. I'll be busy. He slammed his door shut, started the engine, and sped out of the driveway like in the Indy 500.

Guest Book Comments

"We have loved every moment of our stay in your beautiful home."

Chapter 12

The estimate total took me aback. A call to another furnace company for a comparison was in order. I crumpled, then stuffed the problem into my pocket, and headed back to the cellar. I switched on the light where we heard the laughter and discovered a large room. A single bulb hung from the ceiling, revealing remnants of the previous owners. An over-sized wooden workbench sat in the center, its smooth pine surface worn down by years of use. Nail holes, gashes, and hammer dents covered the top. The edge had the indent from the squeeze of a mounted vise. A shelf beside the entrance held long pieces of lumber covered in thick dust, the carpenter long gone. On the opposite wall, several sets of handmade wooden crutches hung in a row, in a progression of sizes from child to adult, an eerie comparison to a growth chart. A wooden wheelchair with a cane seat and back sat below them. The workbench held a cardboard box with old Christmas decorations sticking out. I walked around the table to get a closer look and picked up a small metal reindeer off the top, its brittle brown paint chipped off at my touch. There were several more nestled in among a red sleigh and Santa figure.

I jumped back when something dropped onto my foot, then leaned down, and peeked under the table. There were several wooden boxes with faded company names painted on the sides. A small, brown tooled leather purse lay on the floor by the box in front of my foot. I lifted the box onto the table and then picked up the purse; I clicked it opened and, finding it empty, I laid it on the table and shifted my attention back to the box. I reached in and held up a man's brown wool bathing shorts and then a matching tank top. I laid them on the table and pulled out a woman's navy wool, one-piece swimsuit with an attached knee-length skirt. The style looked to be before the 1920's. The wool felt stiff, but on examination, to my surprise, there were no moth holes. I folded the woman's swimsuit on top of the man's and looked in the box again. At the bottom sat a large black leather purse. I tried to pick it up by the handle, but whatever it held felt too heavy for the cracked leather to hold without tearing. Sliding both hands under to cradle it worked to lift it out and onto the table. I clicked it open and drew in a breath. It contained at least a hundred brass and silver keys. I laid the purse on its side and pulled out bunches at a time until an assortment lay scattered across the table. I picked up small silver one with a round label attached that read "Mary's hatbox," but most of them were door keys. One had a string tag knotted through the open end. I held it out under the light, "Maid's quarters."

"Were these the keys to Sunbrook?" I whispered. I pulled more keys out and a small, brown leather coin purse lay among them. I twisted its tiny clasp at the top, looked inside, and saw a small stubby brass key with a tattered, purple velvet ribbon. Why would someone place it in the coin purse separate from the other keys? It resembled the luggage keys of today, only somewhat larger and sturdier. I looked closer and read the engraved initials *"JCL."*

"John Collin Lloyd, the original owner of Sunbrook," I whispered again. The previous owner had told me that John Lloyd had it built as the family's summer cottage. What the wealthy, at that time, called a home in the country they used to get away from the heat and dirt of the city. His suitcase may be long gone, but finding the key amazed me. I placed it back into the coin purse, held it close to my heart and mouthed a prayer of thanks, then slid all the keys on the table back into the large purse, and laid the little one on top. A cotton flour sack lined the bottom of the wooden box. I pulled it out, laid it open on the table, then lowered the purse down into it. With my treasure secured, I picked the sack up by the top and rested the bottom on my other hand. Then, I rode the elevator up to the second floor. I opened the door and peeked out to make sure I was alone; I stepped out into the empty vestibule and made a swift escape to my bedroom. I wanted to keep my new-found treasure a secret for now. I opened the bottom bureau drawer and hid the keys in the back, under my silk lingerie. I would show them to Mike later, both the keys and the lingerie. As far as I was concerned, it was time to make up. I went down stairs to my office, called another furnace company, and set up an appointment for the next afternoon. Maybe this technician wouldn't be wired so tight and would appreciate the beauty of Sunbrook. Hopefully, he will present me with a lower estimate.

The rest of the day proved to be mine, so I walked into the library and picked up my book from the chair. The estimate in my pocket crinkled as I pulled my feet up and dug into the soft leather. I began to read and even though the book's subject enthralled me, I found myself reading the same paragraph over again. The $25,000 estimate in my pocket nagged at me.

It slipped away when I heard Grace pounding down the stairs. She rushed into the library scowling, with her hands clasped into fists at her side, her lips drawn into a thin line. "Why are you sitting here? Didn't you hear that loud boom?"

"No, I was outside and then in the basement. When did you hear it?"

"I don't know, but it woke me."

"Where did it come from?"

"I'm not sure. I thought something hit the house. I got up and ran around checking for the front of a truck sticking through a hole in the wall. No truck, so I looked in every closet thinking maybe a suitcase full of cannon balls fell off the top shelf."

"It was that loud? Are you sure you weren't dreaming?"

"No, I wasn't dreaming," she said, still scowling.

"Maybe it came from the traffic. An engine could have backfired. A semi-truck and trailer could have made the noise you described if it hit a bump or if its load shifted."

She placed her hands on her hips. "You can keep coming up with these annoying explanations all day; I know it came from inside the house," she raised her voice at me. "I know what I heard."

"Ok, ok," I said, holding my hands up in front of me and backing off. "I believe you. We'll find the cause; we may even hear it again. I'll go down into the basement and look around. Something big may have fallen from the vibrations of the highway."

"There you go with the explanations again." She put her hands on her hips. "Go ahead and look but cover your head—you never know what the vibrations will bring down on it," she said, waving me off.

I took the elevator to the basement, turned on all the lights and checked every room for something heavy that may had fallen. I found nothing and regretted having to go up and report my findings to her. The elevator stopped back on the first floor and I opened the door to find Grace standing there, her hands still on her hips, "Well?"

I stepped out past her and into the kitchen where she followed close behind. I poured a coffee and sat down at the table, "I didn't find anything."

"Well, I think we have a ghost," she started counting on her fingers, "The paint roller noise you heard, the missing dust cloth, the walking wedding gown, and now the loud noise." She put her hands back on her hips and glared at me waiting for my response.

I decided to agree with her because she was quite upset at this point. "I'm guessing that you're right. There is no explanation for all those things that happened."

"I feel better that you believe me, but I'm not

thrilled that the house is haunted."

"I'm sorry, Grace. You aren't going to quit because of this, are you? I really need you and would hate to lose you."

Raising her voice, she looked up and then around the room talking to the air, "I'm not quitting. I'm not afraid of any ghost, and I'll give it hell if it haunts me again."

Guest Book Comments

"Thank you for all your hospitality and superb accommodations."

Chapter 13

The high-pitched tweet coming from my office startled us. Grace had poured our coffee and was sitting at the table, when I returned carrying the cordless.

"You must be feeling better. You didn't go back to bed," I said.

"Yeah, well, I don't feel like being alone right now. Who called?"

"Sharon Carvy, she just booked Sunbrook's first Christmas party. It's in three weeks, on December seventeenth. I planned to decorate for Christmas on the first of December, but I'll start tonight. I'm going up to the third floor to bring down the decorations. Why don't you call and have a pizza delivered?"

I gulped my coffee down and started to leave, but stopped and turned around when Grace yelled, "Wait! Um, um," she looked around at a loss for words, trying to pull them from the air. "Sit and have another cup while I call, and then I'll go up with you." Without waiting for a reply, she grabbed my mug from the counter and poured the coffee.

"Oh…ok, Grace." I frowned and sat down, trying to figure out what made her so jumpy. Then it dawned on me. She's afraid the ghost will show up while she's alone. She set the hot coffee down in front of me. After all of her talk about, "giving the ghost hell," she turned into a timid mouse fearing that at any minute the cat would pounce. Compassion for her welled up in me, replacing judgment. "Sure, Grace, I'll wait until you make the call. The phone's there on the counter." I nodded my head and lifted my mug in a gesture toward it, and then I took a sip.

***

We loaded a few cardboard boxes of green garland, light strands and glass ornaments into the elevator and sent it down to the first floor. Our pizza arrived not long after we unloaded the boxes and stacked them in the foyer. We washed up and sat down to eat.

"You have a lot of decorating to do. Do you think you can get it done in time? You know you'll spend hours decorating and then redecorating to get up to your expectations." She took a big bite of pizza and mumbled, "Just kidding."

Grace's playful jabs at me proved she was in better spirits. "If I work at it a couple of hours every day, it all should be finished by the end of the week," I said.

"I can take care of cleaning the rooms and shopping for groceries if you make up a list. I'm familiar with the brands you use."

"Thanks, Grace, but are you sure you can handle it?" She froze mid-bite, frowned and glared at me. I took a big bite of pizza and mumbled, "Just kidding."

Grace helped me clear the mantles and the tops of book shelves. After we laid all of the pine garlands on top we strung white, twinkle lights through them. "This is as far as I go. The fancy-mancy stuff is all yours," Grace said and bounded up the stairs. She called down over the banister, "I'm taking a sleeping pill, so that nothing disturbs me. Don't try to wake me. I'll be dead to the world. If you need anything, it will have to wait until tomorrow."

After weaving wide, red satin ribbon through the garland and adding assorted colors of shiny glass bulb ornaments, dried hydrangeas, and baby's breath, I stepped back to check my work. The light's reflection in the mirrored bulbs gave the illusion of twice their numbers. I was satisfied with the results of all the shelves—the four fireplaces were next.

The clock in the foyer chimed ten when I had finished tucking the last flower into the garland on the mantel beside it. Mike walked through the back door. He hung up his coat, sat down, and took off his boots. He leaned back in the chair and sighed, staring into space. Watching him from the shadows, my chest grew tight and tears rimmed my eyes. Did buying Sunbrook put an extra burden on Mike? He didn't need any more responsibility and neither did I. My plan to retire at forty and write my novel and his to cut back at work and enjoy his cars would have to wait. I dreamed of living in a large historic home while he was content with our little, paid for, ranch in the suburbs. He said he didn't want to buy Sunbrook, but I wouldn't take no for an answer and wore him down with promises that the bed and breakfast, 2nd Hand Rose, our savings, and his job would be enough to finance our undertaking. It was, but now we're under the pressure of debt again and have added to our work load. But Sunbrook enchanted me from the first moment I saw it. When the realtor opened the front door, a welcoming breath swept over me. Its walls felt alive, and I touched them throughout, laying my hand against its heart, waiting for a beat. The more we walked through the rooms, it pulled me in and wouldn't let go. It had such an uncanny effect on me that by the time we were ready to leave, my decision had been made. Nothing would stop me from making Sunbrook Mansion our home.

"Hey," I said in a soft, intimate tone from the kitchen doorway.

"Hey," he said back in the same tone, walked over, and took me in his arms.

"Are you okay?" I asked. Not wanting to break the spell, I wrapped my arms around his back and pulled him closer, leaning into him.

"Sure. We changed truck tires today. It's a big job. Tires me out." He pulled back, our eyes met, and we both smiled at his pun. He let go of me and said, "I'm going up to shower."

"Give me a couple of minutes to unplug the lights and I'll join you."

"Sure." His eyes lit up, and he reached for me again only brushing my arm since I already moved out of his reach. "I'll light a fire," he said and started up the steps.

I didn't waste any time with the lights and rushed up the stairs to the bedroom.

***

We ate breakfast together before Mike would have to leave for work. By the time Grace joined us, we were so engrossed in each other—we began sending private signals with our eyes across the table. Grace picked up on our little tête-á-tête, rolled her eyes, and said, “Good Lord, you two. Get a room!” She grabbed her cereal bowl and coffee and marched into the dining room, leaving us snickering in her wake.

As Mike pulled out of the driveway, the phone rang. “Hello, Sunbrook Mansion,” I said.

“This is Sharon Carvy. I’m coming up tomorrow at three to show you how I want the rooms set up.”

She caught me off guard with her abrupt demand, and I agreed, forgetting to check my calendar first.

Grace sat at the far end of the dining room. “Sharon, the party girl, called again. She’ll be here at three tomorrow,” I said.

“What for? The party’s not for three weeks.”

“We have to prepare, see how she wants the tables set up and if we need to move any furniture—standard procedure for anyone who books a party.”

“I guess, but you should charge her for your time.”

“It’s in with the price of the party. I set the hourly rate up twenty dollars to compensate.”

“Oh, I see,” she said. “Weren’t you going shopping with Gwen tomorrow?”

“Oh, no, I forgot! That only gives us a couple of hours to eat lunch and shop. I’ll call her and ask if we could meet for breakfast instead.”

“You don’t have to rush home. I’ll be here at three o’clock.”

My mind filled with several scenarios of the collision between Grace and Sharon. Grace would never put up with Sharon's bossy attitude and wouldn't hold back in telling her so, along with a few choice words from her colorful vocabulary. Sharon didn't sound like the type of person who would accept criticism from Grace, even without her obscenities, and my beautiful Christmas decorations would be strewn throughout all the rooms after the cat fight.

"That's ok, Grace. I'll be back by three."

Guest Book Comments

"We had a lovely time at Sunbrook. We look forward to staying again in the future."

Chapter 14

The clock in the foyer chimed half past two, when I stepped through the door. Plenty of time to get my packages put away and refresh my makeup before Sharon arrived. Grace's little red Mazda wasn't parked in its usual place in the driveway, and the note she left for me on the table said that, since I didn't need her, she decided to go Christmas shopping.

Sharon pulled in the driveway right on time. I wrote "prompt" above her name on my clipboard to remind me to be the same in the future. As proof of how efficient Sunbrook was managed, I opened the door before she had a chance to ring. She looked at me, her finger poised toward the button. "Welcome, Sharon. I'm Tiffany."

She rushed in. "Where's the dining room? I want to see how big it is," she said without stopping.

"Straight ahead and…" She disappeared around the corner before I could direct her further, so I hurried to catch up. She stood in the middle of the dining room and watched my face as I approached. I tried to hide my surprise at her rude manner but knew it was without success when her mouth turned up into a slight smirk. She enjoyed rattling people's nerves, one of the traits of a serial killer. Her shrewd tactics would have gotten the best of Grace. Thank heavens for Christmas shopping.

"This is elegant, and the perfect place for my boss's birthday party. I like the historical aspects of the house. I'm sure my guests will like it, too. My list is comprised of many important people in the area," she said, her nose lifting a couple of inches into the air. "There will be around fifty guests, and I'm bringing the food. I'll set it up, but I expect you to replenish the trays throughout the evening. I'll be here about an hour before the party begins. Say around six o'clock. Set up an eight foot food table along this wall and one beside the fireplace, here."

"But…" I started to interrupt. She aimed a challenging glare at me while she planted herself on the spot until I wrote it down and then hustled into the library, "One in front of the window in this room." I followed her taking notes while trying to keep up. "A six foot table in front of this wall," she said from the foyer. "This area is fine as it is." She stood in the door of the music room. "I presume the fireplaces will be lit," she said; narrowing her eyes and setting her mouth in a thin line, she gave me a hard you-better-say-yes stare.

"Yes," I said, but it sounded more like a croak. I cleared my throat. "Of course," I said in a firm, decisive voice. Mustering up some courage, I asked, "Would you like candles? For an extra fee, I could place candelabras with cream tapers on the tables and add assorted heights of pillar candles in the same color around the room."

"Fine, here's a check for the deposit." Not waiting for me to take it, she slapped the check down on my clipboard, almost knocking it out of my hand.

"I'll see you at five o'clock on the seventeenth." With that she walked out, leaving the door wide open in her wake, but before she stepped off the porch, Sunbrook's heavy oak door slammed shut, and the metallic click of the deadbolt echoed all around me.

Guest Book Comments

"We really enjoyed staying in this beautiful Mansion."

Chapter 15

Stunned by Sharon's quick exit and astonished by the door closing and locking before my eyes, my adrenaline pumped, freezing me in place, while my brain scrambled to make sense of it. The slam of a car door drew my attention but seemed distant, on the other side of something… somewhere. The kitchen door opened. The crackle of bags clutched tight and Grace's familiar footsteps brought me a hint of relief. The imagined mist that blurred my sight began to clear, and my tunnel vision to the door melted away. Sunbrook's vast foyer emerged, and I began to recover from the strange phenomenon I had just witnessed.

"What in the world is wrong with you?" Grace asked. "You look like you just saw a ghost." She looked up in a panic, swung around to look behind her, and then positioned herself against the wall, holding her bags up in defense. "Damn it, where is it?" A soft, twinkling laugh of a woman filled the room. "Was that a laugh? Did the ghost just laugh at me?" Her insulted ego brought courage to the forefront, and Grace stepped away from the wall. Not knowing where to look, her head jerked from me, to the air, back to me, and to the air again. She reminded me of a clucking chicken. "Listen lady, I won't put up with being laughed at," she said, raising her voice.

"You're...... comical," the specter's reply surrounded us.

Abandoning courage, Grace jumped close beside me and scrunched down, covering her head with her arm, two shopping bags dangled in front of her face. "Holy hell, she talked to me!"

"Who are you?" I asked the ghost, anxious for an answer, but only silence followed. "Why are you here?" Still silence. "Well anyway, we're glad you're here."

"Like hell, we are," Grace said.

"Sshhh," I said with my finger to my lips. We stayed still for a few more minutes before I shrugged to Grace. "I guess she's gone."

"Yah, well, good riddens," she said and then stood up to her full height. "Will you go upstairs with me while I put these packages in my room?" She held up her shopping bags. Two red splotches on the apples of her cheeks emphasized her ashen face. I wondered if my skin looked as pale as hers.

"Sure, Grace."

***

We decided to go to Perkins restaurant for supper. We both needed to get out of the house for a while.

"How'd it go with the party girl, Sharon, right?"

"Oh, it went well." I stopped there and took a bite of my salad, avoiding eye contact, then glanced up to see her looking at me, waiting for more information. "She's a no nonsense kind of person, very efficient. She sure didn't waste any of my time, or hers." I paused and took another bite. Grace still stared at me, ignoring her salad. "She's bringing all the food.

We don't even have to supply the dishes and flatware, she's bringing that too. Easy cleanup, this party will be a breeze."

"What are you not telling me?" Grace asked, her brow furrowed, giving me a side look.

"Like I said, she didn't waste any time, but she let me know that she's used to getting her way." Then, I lowered my voice to a whisper. "The ghost didn't like that Sharon was rude and dismissive with me, so as soon as she stepped out the door to leave, the ghost slammed and locked it behind her."

"Whoa, no way," Grace said, leaning back away from me, eyes wide.

"Lower your voice, Grace!" I glanced around to see if we drew any attention from the other diners, but everyone seemed to be involved in their own conversations.

"The ghost must like you, looks like she's got your back, too." Her body shivered. "She makes me nervous as hell." Then her face lit up in revelation. "Hey, will you put in a good word for me? I could use some spirit magic."

"Let's eat and talk about something else. How's your mother?" I asked, ignoring Grace's question. We relaxed, took our time, and enjoyed our salads before leaving.

The telephone rang when we walked in the door. "Grace, we have a guest checking in tomorrow for two nights. I'll be at 2nd Hand Rose all day."

"No problem, I'll be here."

"Great, I'm going upstairs! Goodnight, Grace."I did a special prep for bed, and after I powdered and perfumed, I knelt down and opened my lingerie drawer to pick out something alluring to wear for Mike. Surprised to see the small, black coin purse lying on top, I pushed aside delicate puffs of chiffon, lace, and satin. The large purse still lay at the bottom, with the latch closed, just as I left it. My mind on Mike and the lingerie, I stuffed the coin purse back inside the large one and pulled out a royal blue, satin nightgown with spaghetti straps, and slipped it over my head. The smooth fabric slid down my body, its high hem stopping a few inches below the top of my thigh. "*Short enough to be interesting but long enough to cover the subject,*" came to mind. That's what my sexist high school typing teacher used to say, about the length of our skirts. Well, in this case it's okay. I'm not an innocent high school sophomore. My mirror reflected a mature and, although not perfect, voluptuous woman, waiting for her loving husband, wearing one of his favorite colors. She knew she would enrapture him with her smooth, creamy skin, glowing like the moon against a rich, twilight sky.

Guest Book Comments

"It has been a delightful, relaxing stay."

Chapter 16

"Sunbrook Mansion Bed and Breakfast, Tiffany speaking."

"Hi, Tiffany, this is Coleen Martin from the Hollidaysburg Women's Club. Is it too late to book a Christmas party? We're hoping the evening of Saturday, the tenth is available.

"Yes, that date is open. When would you like to get together to see Sunbrook and make all the arrangements?"

"We could come Thursday afternoon at one o'clock. There will be four of us, if that's okay?"

"That sound great, Colleen! I'll see you then."

"We're looking forward to it. Thank you so much, goodbye," she said with excitement in her voice.

Colleen sounded like she would be a pleasure to work with. "I hope her companions are nice, too," I said out loud while jotting down her name and number on the tenth. The sweet scent of jasmine filled my office making me smile. "We don't need any more slamming doors, do we?" I said, looking up. A mischievous chuckle surrounded me. My own laughter bubbled up to join in until I looked down to see, lying next to the telephone, the second thermostat estimate staring up at me.

"Grace, what did the furnace technician say?" I

asked, holding up the estimate.

"He's hot," she said, fanning her face with the dish towel.

"He said he's hot?" I asked, being sarcastic.

"No! I said he's hot. You should hire him."

"He's not a play toy, Grace. I'm not going to hire him because he's good looking."

"No, he's hot!" Grace said, now fanning the towel in double time. "Besides, he liked Sunbrook, and the ghost didn't haunt him. I'll bet she thinks he's hot, too."

"Oh, Grace," I said, examining the document. "This estimate is $200.00 less than the first one. It's still going to take a big chunk out of my savings account. But I want my guests to be comfortable." Feeling overwhelmed, I shook my head to clear it. "Mike and I will compare them this weekend and then decide. I'm going to 2nd Hand Rose now."

***

Gwen was at the computer entering the week's sales.

"Hi Gwen," I said, putting my lunch in the refrigerator. "Need some help with those?"

"No, I'm almost finished. We had a busy week."

"That's good," I said, staring into space.

"What's wrong? You look preoccupied." She walked over to me and studied my face. "Something's worrying you. What happened? That Sharon woman hasn't been bullying you again, has she?"

"No, but I did want to ask if you would help me with her party. Grace is going on a shopping excursion to the Lancaster outlets with her sisters."

"Sure, I'll help. It would be a pleasure to put 'Ms. Sharon the terrible' in her place if she gives us any lip. Now tell me what's really bothering you?"

"Well, I'm concerned about spending a quarter of my savings so soon after opening Sunbrook. The business is still in its infancy and won't be making a profit anytime soon. What if this isn't the only unexpected expense? What if something else happens to deplete our nest egg? My voice quivered. "What if I can't pay the bills and I lose Sunbrook?" The thought left me speechless. Feeling defeated, I plopped down onto the nearest chair, my shoulders dropped and my body deflated with the release of a huge sigh that left me leaning forward, staring at the floor.

Gwen pulled up a chair in front of me. She sat down and lifted my limp hands. Her firm grip made me sit up and give her my full attention. "You've got yourself all worked up over something that hasn't even happened, and worrying about it isn't going to get you anywhere."

"Yes, but what if…" I started, but she interrupted refusing to listen to what she knew would be another negative monologue.

"Listen to me, this is the reason you set up the business account, and spending a portion to make your customers happy is a win, win. Happy customers tell other potential customers about Sunbrook, which makes your business and your savings grow." She smiled as her voice ended in an uplifting lilt.

"I guess you're right. I did get another Christmas party call this morning," I said, hearing the same rise in my voice.

"See, there's already a reason to be hopeful. I'm sure you'll get more party bookings and guests calling to stay. Word of mouth is the best advertisement and besides, how could anyone resist Sunbrook?"

"You're right, Gwen. I'll call the furnace company, after I talk to Mike, and have them start work as soon as possible. I feel much better now that I've made a decision. Thanks for pulling me out of my doldrums. Your encouragement to get control of my thoughts and take charge of the situation is what I needed."

This wasn't the first time Gwen has been able to help me see things from a different perspective. When our bid for Sunbrook turned into a bidding war, the owner accepted the other offer, and I thought I lost my dream. Anger, sadness, and then an-apathy for my everyday life left me lethargic, forgetful, and scatter brained. Even simple decisions became difficult. Gwen listened for days, while I complained about how the owner made the wrong choice and then whined about what should have been. She let me go on until one day she put up her hand, palm so close to my face, my eyes crossed. The move made me pull back my head and stop, my mouth hanging open in mid-sentence. "Listen, I understand that you believe Sunbrook should be yours, but the owner didn't choose you, and there is nothing you can do, except stop wallowing and pray. After all, the papers aren't signed yet."

My eyes darted back and forth, as one word at a time soaked into my one-track mind before forming into sentences that made sense. Then my thoughts sifted out the golden words. "Pray. The papers aren't signed yet." Joy burst from my heart when the realization that there was still hope became apparent. So I prayed, and a week later my realtor called—the pending buyers changed their minds and, if I still wanted it, Sunbrook was mine.

Gwen and I sat holding hands a moment longer before she looked at the wall clock. "Ten o'clock," she said and then jumped up, pulling me with her. She fished the door keys from her pocket and started walking toward the front of the store. "Time to unlock the doors and let the money in,"

I pushed back a bundle of clothes on a rack and examined a blouse to be priced, listening to Gwen's vibrant, gracious voice, "Good morning, welcome to 2nd Hand Rose. Who told you about us? Oh yes, she's one of our many loyal customers."

Guest Book Comments

"I had enjoyed being here! Breakfast was more than I could eat and scrumptious!"

Chapter 17

The numerous envelopes felt light in my hand but weighed heavily on my mind. This month's bills were paid and ready to mail. The pair of estimates sat on my desk; their inflated amounts taunted me. I couldn't help but wonder that if we could meet this expense, maybe, just maybe the worst would be behind us, and the bed and breakfast would start to pay off. The day after the furnace technician gave us the second estimate, the company called and told me it didn't include electrical. They recommended an electrician to call and set up the appointment for an estimate on wiring and hookups. That additional worry made my spirits plummet deeper. Then I remembered Gwen's pep talk. *Well, all I can do is advertise and pray for a full calendar of guests as well as wedding and party bookings.* The foyer doorbell chimed. "Yes, a guest has arrived!" I glanced out the window and saw her striking blond head turned toward the driveway. I dropped the mail into the out box and forced a smile—my weapon to remove and leave my worried face at my desk.

Her long smooth mane bounced and shimmered when she jumped at the click of the door latch. She turned around and smiled. "Hi, I'm Sheila Rodgers." Her flawless peach-tinted complexion revealed her age at no more than thirty. The casual lemon-yellow blouse hugged her narrow waist and complemented emerald-green eyes fringed with long dark lashes. She walked through the foyer, pulling a suitcase at her side. "I made reservations for the weekend. Has my friend, Cullen arrived yet?" Her eyes sparkled when she mentioned his name, then her gaze wandered up the staircase as she leaned forward in anticipation of his appearance at the top. "He's coming from Baltimore." She placed mango-manicured fingers on her décolletage. "I'm from Columbus. We're meeting here," she said, while walking back to the door where she searched up and down the driveway through the window.

"Cullen hasn't arrived yet, but until he does, why don't I show you to your room where you can freshen up and relax until he gets here."

"Oh, of course!" Disappointment dulled the sparkle in her eyes. "It has been a long drive. That sounds like a good idea." Reluctant to leave the window, she lingered a few more seconds before joining me at the staircase. She took one last look at the door and then followed. "I'm sorry to keep you waiting; it's just that we haven't been together for a while."

"I understand. What's he driving?" I climbed sideways to make sure she continued in my wake.

"A silver Volvo SUV," she said, leaning her head out over the railing toward the door. The longing in her eyes tugged at my heart, which prompted me to send Cullen a mental reprimand, along with an order to *GET HERE NOW!*

"I'll let you know as soon as I see him pull into

the driveway." I opened the door to her room and stepped aside. "I've reserved the Deborah room for you; it's one of our most luxurious with a spa bathroom and private balcony."

Sheila walked past me as she glanced around the room. She stopped at the king size bed, sat and smoothed her palm across the white Egyptian-cotton comforter, and then she gazed up at me, smiled, and said, "It's perfect."

Thrilled and empowered by Shelia's *perfect* satisfaction, I rushed down the first set of stairs, twirled across the landing, and then with a slow graceful decent raised my hand in an elegant royal wave to the bottom and all the way to my office.

***

I had just emailed the last ad to the State College newspapers when the front of the silver Volvo appeared and moved at a slow speed down the driveway. I rushed up to the room and, as soon as I knocked, the door jerked open. Shelia dashed past me and disappeared in a flash down the steps. I followed and reached the foyer in time to look out and see their bodies collide. Sheila, on tiptoe, wrapped her arms around Cullen's neck. He embraced her and their mouths met in a long ravenous kiss, the car door still open. I ducked into my office and watched them from the window. Voyeurism has never been my forté. I've fostered complete respect for my guests' privacy, but Shelia's anticipation of Cullen's arrival and the deflated look on her face at his absence ignited my protective instincts. But, to avoid the embarrassment of being discovered, I stood back from the window. After a few more kisses, he touched her cheek, their eyes locked for a moment, and then he pulled a small suitcase from the back seat. They walked side by side to the door, their arms looped around each other's waist. I closed the office door as they drew near and then waited for the sound of their footsteps on the stairs before emerging to inquire. "Excuse me, what time would you like breakfast?"

"How about 10:30?" Cullen said, his eyes never leaving Sheila's. She nodded and without pause, they continued to the top where she took his hand and drew him into the bedroom.

I mumbled to myself, "Alrighty then," as Grace would say after a similar encounter.

***

"Those are the guests who checked in this morning," I told Grace as we finished eating supper in the kitchen. I pointed to the couple strolling across the parking lot. "Those two are really in love."

Cullen's large palm lay on the small of Sheila's back. He paused, pulled her close and pressed a gentle kiss on her eyes, then the tip of her nose and then moved his mouth over her pouty bow-shaped lips. Her lips welcomed his as she clung to him, sliding her hands over his wide muscular back and then down to his narrow waist. Sheila pulled her head back and said something to Cullen as she inserted her fingers into the back slit pockets of his navy slacks.

"Whew!" Grace picked up her napkin and fanned her face. "It looks like they can't keep their hands off of each other, like another couple I know." She raised her eyebrows up and down at me.

I flashed side eyes at her, stood, and picked up our dirty plates before we both turned our attention back to Cullen and Shelia. He had opened her car door, but before getting in she pulled Cullen's head down into another lingering kiss. Grace fanned faster while I tried to force my gaze from the scene, stumbling to the sink.

***

I lit the fireplace then primped and slipped into my sheerest negligee, which matched my bright red lipstick. I leaned against the bed with one hand on my hip and the other stroking the top of the smooth brass footboard while striking my sexiest pose. Mike opened the door; the shower steam filled the room behind him. "Wow!" was all he could say before I pulled him into a fierce hug and claimed his mouth with mine. I pulled him to the bed and pushed him down falling on top of him. With my knees on each side of his hips and my hands by his head, I straightened my arms to look at him. "Our weekend guests are a hot-for-each-other couple with a request for two late breakfasts, which makes two late nights for us.

***

On the last morning of Sheila and Cullen's stay, Grace had pulled the hot cinnamon buns from the oven while I set the fruit plate and juice on a tray. We sat with our coffee listening for their voices on the stairs. When our mugs were empty, I filled them again.

"Well, I think it's rude to be this late. What's

with them anyway? They should have been down a half hour ago. The cinnamon rolls are going to dry out if they sit in the oven much longer." Grace stood and started pacing before she walked over and opened the oven door a few inches and peeked in. "They'll start to get hard, too." Frustrated, she let go of the handle causing the door to spring shut with a bang. "Come on, people, we have a life, too!"

My shoulders rose as I cringed. "Grace, stop making a commotion. You don't have to wait, I can cook and serve breakfast. Aren't you going to your mother's today?"

"Yes, she's expecting me at 12:30." She looked at the ceiling. "Hey, you two up there, that's 12:30 pm not am."

"Keep it down, Grace! I said you can go get ready. I'll take care of this."

"Well, okay—but Tiffany shouldn't have to do this alone," she said to the ceiling again, her voice rising up a scale with each word.

"Git!" I said and pointed toward the foyer.

"I'm outta here." She bounced out of the kitchen and pounded up the stairs.

I let out a deep sigh and slid the newspaper from across the table. And read. After fifteen minutes, I stopped to place their lukewarm fruit plate and juice back into the fridge then opened the oven and pinched a cinnamon roll off with my finger. *They're still moist, but for how long?* Concerned for their freshness, I grabbed a pot holder and moved the pan to the warming drawer below. Their delectable aroma encircled my head. *Mm, might as well have one with my coffee.* I topped my mug, sat, and delighted in the smooth creamy icing and warm cinnamon dough melting on my tongue, their sweetness exploding over my taste buds. I took my time, savoring each morsel to the last bite. I entertained having another when the clock in the foyer chimed, bringing my attention to the kitchen clock. *Twelve o'clock! Where are they?* I decided to find out.

***

I stopped at the top of the steps reluctant to go any further to knock on their door. "Grace wouldn't have a problem with knocking—I wish I were more like her," I mumbled. Then I shook my head. "Wait a minute! What am I thinking?" I shudder at the thought.

This is ridiculous! It's past check out, and I have to have the room cleaned for the next guest arriving at four o'clock. Grace is right, they are being rude. But the thought still didn't give me the courage to disturb them. Then I remembered that my room adjoined theirs. I'll listen through the wall and then knock if I hear them moving around. I opened my door and began to tip-toe across when a vision on the balcony through the sheer curtains at my window stopped me. My heels dropped. Overwhelming awe swept away all thoughts of rudeness and stale cinnamon rolls.

My heart swelled with joy as my fingers pressed over my smile at the sight of my guests. They were dancing! A love song played from their retro boom box perched on the balcony railing. Their bodies swayed to the slow tempo of the music. Cullen touched her face with his fingertips. She held her gaze on him as a single tear slipped from the corner of her eye. His thumb slid over her cheek bone wiping it away. He pressed his mouth to her brow and then to where the tear had trailed; her lips parted, and he placed a gentle kiss on them. She tilted her head back as his moved down and nuzzled her neck. Then he drew her close and she nestled against his chest, her eyes closed. They clung to each other as if it was their last embrace.

My heart burst with pride as I witnessed Sunbrook's enchantment over the couple—its balcony setting sparking a romantic moment that it had conjured up from the past. But the moment was bittersweet. They would be separated soon, so they clung to each other, reluctant to depart.

***

I watched from the kitchen window as Cullen offered Sheila his hand and she placed her fingers within as they walked to her car. He opened the back of her SUV, lifted her suitcase inside, and closed the lid. He pulled her close and buried his face in her hair. She wrapped her arms around his waist and snuggled against him. They stood like that as if they were the only two people in the world. Then he pulled back and, with his hand, tilted her chin up, so their eyes met before their lips joined in a long passionate kiss. When it was over, he released her, and they both backed away toward their car. Sheila opened her car door, brushed the tears now trailing down her face, and then slid behind the wheel as Cullen did. Both cars started and pulled out of the driveway—one off to Baltimore, the other to Columbus.

Guest Book Comments

"We loved our stay, especially the balcony. Sunbrook is enchanting and so romantic."

Chapter 18

Exhaustion consumed me at the end of the day at 2nd Hand Rose. A first time customer had spent the last three hours shopping. She stood in front of Jane, our cashier, watching her ring up and pack the tenth bag with her selections. "This store is great. You have a vast array of quality merchandise, and your prices are reasonable. I bought ten complete outfits, with accessories, and most of them had designer labels."

"Yes, we have many consignors who only bring in designer, and new items arrive every day," Gwen said.

"I can't wait to come back next week. Oh, I hope I don't miss anything until then." She said, stomping her foot and turning to look around the store; with furrowed brows raised, her eyes scanned the racks with longing.

Gwen picked up an art deco table lamp off the counter. "Jane and I will help you carry your purchases to your car." Gwen held the door open for her and Jane and then trailed out behind them.

"I have the perfect spot for that lamp in my sun room." The customer's voice faded as the door swished shut.

***

After listening to her glowing review, "Happy customers make your savings grow," came to mind.

Gwen's words to me were all I needed to continue to dispel my worry of Sunbrook's repairs and walk with a lighter step. Gwen and Jane walked back in through the front door. "I tallied the cash drawer. Here's the money bag," I said, handing it to Gwen. "It's time for me to run. I'm serving a guest breakfast, so I'll be late tomorrow. Happy customers make your savings grow," I said, giving Gwen a grateful hug. "Thanks for your encouragement. "I won't forget it. See you tomorrow."

***

With the thought still swimming around in my head, I almost collided with Grace at the kitchen door. We both jumped back. Her eyes widened with surprise. Then she whizzed past me. "Where are you going in such a hurry?" I asked.

"Mom's! We're picking up my sisters and going to the Mishler Theatre to see, *The Sound Of* Music; curtain's up in forty-five minutes. Jack checked in. He's at supper. Breakfast at eight," she yelled the cliff notes without turning while jetting to her car.

"Okay! Thanks, Grace. Have a good time." I barely finished my sentiment before she slammed her car door, started the engine, and sped out of the driveway. The *Sound Of Music* is her favorite movie, so I wasn't surprised by her whirlwind departure to see the musical. Feeling too tired to eat a meal, I grabbed a yogurt and water from the fridge and then poured a hand full of cashews from the bag, before dragging myself up the stairs to my room. My bed invited me in with its soft, luscious comforter and abundant pillows. My body sank into the waves of satin. After settling in with the TV turned to the news channel, I ate my small fare. It didn't take long, with my hunger appeased and the lull of the newscaster's voice, for my lids to grow heavy and close. The sound of footsteps across the wood floor of the vestibule propelled my eyes open. The room glowed in mellow orange tones, changing shape as the sun disappeared behind the mountain. The clock's bright numbers read six forty-five. My nap must have been a short one. No more than fifteen minutes. The footsteps had to be Jack returning from supper. Rising from the bed, I pinned up my hair at the vanity before going down to prep the fruit and coffee for the morning. My hand jerked at a knock on my bedroom door, scratching my scalp with a bobby pin. While instinct prompted me to rub the spot to alleviate the pain, I opened up the door.

"Hi Tiffany, I'm sorry to disturb you. I'm Jack. Grace told me to knock on your door if I needed anything," he said, shifting from one foot to the other.

"Yes, of course, you're not disturbing me. Is there a problem?"

"Well, I was wondering if I could get some towels. There aren't any in my room."

My cheeks grew hot with embarrassment. "Oh, forgive me! I'll get your towels right away. I rushed around him to the linen closet in the hall, pulled out three fresh bath sheets, washcloths, and hand towels.

"Here, I can take them," he reached out and lifted the pile from my arms.

"I'm terribly sorry for your inconvenience," I said, recalling Grace's hast in leaving to see the

Sound Of Music. Regardless, she wouldn't have forgotten the towels. She always rechecks her work to make sure everything is clean and in its place.

"No problem, but I'm glad you were here, or I would have been searching through all your closets looking for them. Everything is so neat. You could've had a mess on your hands after I'd been through them." He sported a sheepish smile. "My wife says that things are always in turmoil after I've been routing through our closets or drawers looking for something." We both laughed which helped to relieve some of my anxiety.

"Please, feel free to get extra towels anytime you need them. Although, I'll double check to make sure that you have clean ones before you come back from work tomorrow."

"Thanks, but I don't mind. I know how things can get overlooked, even in a well-run enterprise like yours."

"Thank you for the compliment and your understanding," I said, flattered, the heat in my cheeks returned.

"You're welcome! Have a nice evening," he said before walking back to his room.

The ghost may have played this trick on Jack, and the fact that he was a first time guest in town on business worried me. He wouldn't want anything to interfere with his job, like annoying pranks, which could encourage him to look for accommodations elsewhere. A silent prayer of hope passed my lips. Hope that, for once, Grace forgot the towels.

Cynthia Taylor Billotte

Guest Book Comments

"We had a warm and welcoming stay. Thank you for your hospitality."

Chapter 19

The uncut fruit lay on the counter. My knife sliced through the kiwi in smooth, easy strokes. The repetition calmed my nerves. I worked slow and steady until Grace's car pulled in the driveway. The minute she walked in the door, I gave her the Jack report.

"You mean she took every towel that I put in Jack's bathroom this morning?" She stood before me with her hands on her hips, her mouth drawn into a thin line.

"I was hoping you were going to tell me you forgot to put them in his room. The loss of a repeat guest because of the ghost would cause a lapse in the revenue needed to pay Sunbrook's bills," I said, fighting back tears.

"I have an idea. I'll search the rooms for signs of ghost-tampering while you're checking in the guests. It may discourage her from pulling anymore shenanigans."

"Thanks, Grace. That would make me feel much better. I'm going to finish up here and turn in. Working at 2nd Hand Rose and dealing with the ghost have me worn out. I'll see you around 5:00 a.m. Oh, by the way Grace, did you enjoy the musical?"

"Yes, it was *fa-a-antastic!* Such talented actors with beautiful voices! The whole production was incredible. I didn't want it to end." She started humming "Edelweiss" and waltzed around the kitchen with her arms out, holding an imaginary partner.

"That's great, Grace. Now waltz up to your room and get some sleep." I laughed when, without missing a step, she exited the kitchen and continued to glide up the stairs. My neck and back muscles eased with Grace's humorous adieu, along with the satisfaction of my completed task before me. The colorful orange, kiwi, and strawberry arrangement had the serene effect of a kaleidoscope ready to change pattern with a turn of the plate. Now time to take my own advice and get to bed. After double checking my work, my feet took the stairs almost as light and carefree as Grace and her phantom dance partner. At the top jasmine wafted from our bedroom. Frustrated that our door hung open, after being adamant about keeping it closed to protect our privacy, I threw my hands up into the air. What was the ghost up to now? Light filled the room when I slammed my fist against the switch. My hand stayed glued to the wall and my foot froze mid-step when I recognized the small coin purse lying on the bed. Its rough black pebble leather lay in contrast to the smooth satin of the cream comforter. "What is it with this thing?" I asked the ghost out loud.

"Who are you talking to?"

My heart skipped a beat as I let out a yelp and sprung around to see Mike leaning against the doorway, his arms crossed in front of him. "You startled me. You should have made yourself known before speaking. Why would you sneak up behind me like that?" I plopped down on my vanity bench, lay my hand on my chest, and worked to steady my breathing.

"I'm sorry. I knew you had a guest and, not wanting to wake anyone, I came up in my stocking feet." He bent down and picked up his boots from the floor beside him. The muscles in his arm and chest flexed. My breath caught in my throat. "So who *were* you talking to?" He asked again, smiling, his eyes twinkled.

My stomach tingled when teasing turned to desire as his eyes raked up and down my body. "The ghost," I said. My breath quickened when he moved toward me. He hooked one muscular arm around my waist, lifted me to my feet pulling me against him, and his lips came down on mine in a lingering kiss. He leaned his head back. Our eyes locked. "There is no such thing as ghosts. Accompany me in the shower?" He asked.

Left speechless by his kiss and the passion in his heavenly eyes so close to mine, I nodded. He gave me a peck on the lips, released me, and walked into the bathroom. Mesmerized, and unable to move, I glanced over at the tiny black spot on the bed. Anxious to join Mike, I rushed over, snatched up the purse, and gave it a haphazard pitch into the lingerie drawer. Then I stripped off my clothes, almost falling in my haste, composed myself, and sashayed into the bathroom.

***

My eyes opened to the subtle darkness of a five

o'clock dawn. I slipped out of bed and dressed in the walk-in closet, as not to wake Mike.

The batter for the ginger muffins sat on the counter, ready for pouring. Grace came down at five-thirty with a sheepish look on her face. "My alarm didn't go off—ghost trickery, I'm sure." She washed her hands, spooned the mixture into the muffin tin, then slid it into the hot oven.

"Everything's ready! How about some coffee?" I asked, holding the pot over her big "G" mug.

"Yes, please." She waited until I poured, her fingers laced through the handle, before taking it with her to the table. She plopped down in the chair and hunched over the steaming liquid. "We've got to have a talk with Sunbrook's roving spirit about her annoying pranks. She's getting under my skin."

"We will as soon as we tell Mike about her when he comes down."

"You haven't told him yet? What are you waiting for?"

"We-e-ll, I d-i-id," I said, stretching out my words. She rolled her eyes.

"I know, you both were distracted before he could react."

"Well," I hesitated, and she rolled her eyes again. "He said there was no such thing as ghosts before we—I mean he got into the shower." I stopped there when she shoved her hand in front of my face, turning her head away. My face grew hot. I jumped up from the table and scurried around the kitchen looking for a distraction.

"TMI, TMI," Grace said, moving her STOP hand

sign around following me to and fro. We both paused to listen to footsteps coming down the stairs.

"Jack's early. The muffins need five more minutes," I said in a panic. "Quick, help me load the tray." Grace ran over and placed the coffee butler on the tray while I added the fruit plate and orange juice pitcher from the fridge. "This should satisfy him until the muffins are ready," I said, as I picked up the tray and headed to the dining room. "Good morning, Jack. Please, have a seat, and I'll pour your coffee." He complied, rubbing his palms together. "Good morning! This is great." His eager eyes scanned the table while he shifted his weight in the chair, preparing to dig in.

"Thank you! Grace made you fresh ginger mini muffins. I'll bring them in as soon as they're ready. We're also serving pumpkin pancakes and sausage this morning."

"Sounds delicious." He picked up his fork and speared a strawberry, kiwi, and orange as he poured cream into his coffee.

"I'll be right back! Enjoy." Pleased with his vigorous appetite, my step grew light on my way back to the kitchen. Grace handed me a crystal bowl of steaming muffins nestled inside a pale yellow, linen napkin. "Beautiful! Am I detecting a bit of perfection in your presentation, Grace?" Her cheeks turned pink as she waved her hand motioning me away. "Does someone I know have an infatuation with a guest?"

"No comment…now go. I have pancakes and sausage to cook."

Mike appeared in the doorway. We mirrored an intimate, lover's smile, and he winked. Turning toward the dining room, holding my hand close to my chest out of Grace's view, I gave him a secret wave while passing to deliver Jack's muffins.

Grace stood at the stove pouring batter onto the griddle. Several sausage links sizzled along the side. My impatience to join Mike at the table had me tapping my foot for the thirty seconds it took to heat my coffee. I stared through the glass window of the microwave, watching my cup carousel until the annoying beep sounded at the end of the digital count down. With hot coffee in hand, I tiptoed to the table.

"Mike, I'll cook your pancakes as soon as I finish Jack's," Grace said as she flipped them to reveal their golden brown side.

"I'm in no hurry. The truck we're working on isn't scheduled to arrive until nine o'clock."

She squeezed tongs around three links of the cooked sausage, transferred them to a heated dish beside the griddle, and then slid her spatula under the pancakes lifting them on until they towered beside the sausage. "This is ready to serve." Grace directed at me while she set the steaming bountiful plate on the tray with a small crystal carafe of warmed maple syrup and a bowl of fresh whipped cream.

"I'll be right back," I said, before springing off my chair, anxious to serve the main course and return to have breakfast with Mike. But Jack asked a few questions about the mansion and answering them delayed my return. Grace sat in my seat across from Mike with a satisfied smile on her face as she watched him shovel in the pancakes and sausage that she had set before him. Without saying a word, I sat down with my arms crossed, pouting because this chair sat further away from Mike at the end of the table.

"Listen Mike! We gotta talk." He stopped eating to look at her; his mouth full, he gave her a silent nod. Grace stretched her neck out to look at both doors leading into the kitchen. Then she leaned closer to Mike and whispered, "We have a ghost."

Guest Book Comments

"Thanks for the trip back in time. What a memorable way to spend our anniversary."

Chapter 20

"There's no such thing as ghosts," Mike said, picked up a knife, and sliced up one of the sausage links on his plate.

"Oh, yes! There is, and one lives here. I mean one died here.... but she's not dead....well she's dead but....Oh, hell...we have a ghost," Grace said, throwing her hands up in the air. Mike furrowed his brow and shifted his eyes before he looked over at me.

"It's true," I said. "Things have gone missing and then would show up later in a different location. We've heard strange noises in the night."

"And what about the loud boom I heard in broad daylight—ghosts do that, yah know—saw it on TV. And when the ghost made fun of me for being scared of her?" With this memory, Grace cowered and glanced around the kitchen. Mike watched her, smiled, and then followed her eyes before he shook his head and resumed eating.

"I think the ghost took the towels from Jack's bathroom last evening. Grace is certain that she put them there, but Jack knocked on my door saying he didn't have any towels."

"Ah, come on! You two don't believe a ghost took them, do you?" Mike looked back and forth at us. "Grace, maybe you got busy with something else and forgot," he said.

"No, I'm positive I did. I remember dropping one and then taking care to recreate the tri-fold that your wife is so fussy about." She flashed a side glimpse at me to see my reaction.

"Grace, that towel should have been washed again before a guest used it," I said, planting my hands on my hips and boring a glare into her. Her eyes averted, she ignored my attempt to intimidate her.

Mike ignored me, too. "There has to be some kind of explanation. This house can't be haunted. There's no such thing as ghosts," Mike raised his voice, growing louder with each sentence.

"Shhh, keep it down. I don't want Jack to know. It might scare him away, and then he won't come back. He just told me in the dining room that he took off his socks and laid them on his shoes last night, and this morning they weren't there," I said. Mike shook his head back and forth, his face wrinkled with skepticism, his mouth shut tight.

"Listen, I think I hear Jack going upstairs. Well, we aren't getting anywhere here. I guess I'll go clean up the dining room," Grace said. She jumped up and rushed out with a large tray flapping against her thigh.

Mike continued to eat in silence. After adding the last pancake to a plate and refreshing our coffee, I moved to my original seat, closer to him. He pushed his empty dish aside, slid his cup close in front of him, then wrapped his fingers around it, and leaned forward. "These ghost stories are ridiculous, and there's an explanation for every one of them that I'm sure will be revealed with time." I opened my mouth to disagree. "And," he said, holding up his hand, "From now on, I don't want to hear any more about a ghost from either of you. The subject is closed." We both sat in silence while we sipped our coffee before Mike threw back his last gulp and stood. "I gotta go. Dad asked me to pick up the parts for the truck we're working on today."

His adamant closure about the ghost puzzled me. He seemed angry that we brought it up. Or did the possibility of seeing or experiencing any strange phenomenon frighten him? He won't watch scary movies with me but would make fun when I covered my eyes during a commercial for the popular zombie television shows. I'll bet that's how he hides his fear, by making fun of me.

"I won't mention the ghost again. Please, don't leave with a rift between us," I pleaded, blocking the door.

The stern lines on his face disappeared. He placed his hands on my upper arms and leaned his head down nibbling at my neck. "Never," he breathed into my ear. My eyes drooped closed, and my body melted at his gentle touch. He captured my lips in a soft lingering kiss and, while my feet moved on their own, he slowly pivoted me away from the door. He released me, leaving me teetering, breathless before him. I blinked open my eyes to find his face close to mine, his eyes shining with amusement. "I better go before Grace catches us," he said, tilting his head toward the dining room. "I'll see you tonight." He winked and then slid sideways out the door, pulling it closed behind him.

The distant click of the portico door closing caught my attention. Jack appeared outside the kitchen window walking across the driveway toward his black Navigator. He raised his hand in a discreet wave in Mike's direction. Mike returned Jack's greeting with a slight nod before his pickup leapt forward accelerating out of view.

Grace bustled in balancing the tray stacked with delicate china and crystal that clinked and rattled with each step. She reached the sink where she slid the tray across the counter. My shoulders hunched in a cringe when it stopped with a jolt against the backsplash, toppling the crystal pitcher onto one of my best English tea cups. They both exploded into hundreds of tiny shards, sparkling through the air, sending rainbows of color to settle everywhere.

My face grew hot and my body grew rigid; hands balled into fists at my side. "Grace, how could you be so careless? Any normal person would know that's not how you handle fragile glassware. You're always in a rush, slamming things around like your attitude is, 'they're not mine, so what does it matter? Tiffany owns a mansion; she's got money to replace them.' Well news flash, Grace, Tiffany doesn't have the money."

Grace turned toward me. My breath caught in my throat, ending my rant. Tiny specks of blood dotted her face, neck, and arms. The dots grew into droplets that flowed down, leaving thin scarlet trails before they dripped off peppering the golden Georgia pine floor with miniature red polka dots.

"Oh, my God, Grace!" I yelled, leaping around the counter to her side. "No, don't touch your face." I held my up my hands blocking hers from her cuts. "I'll call nine-one-one."

She twisted her arms to study her wounds while I punched the numbers into the phone.

"No, I'll be alright. It's just a little blood."

"911, what's your emergency?"

"It's okay, Grace; they're on the line."

***

Four hours later, I pulled my car back into the garage. "Don't move. I'll get the door," I said, opening my own. I rushed around the long body of my classic Cadillac to the other side and pulled open the door wide. Grace struggled to get out, moaning with pain. Resisting the urge to reach out to help her, I stood back holding the door steady while she used the top as a crutch to pull herself up. She leaned against the side for a minute and then hobbled into the kitchen and up the stairs.

"You rest. I'll bring you some tea and toast," I said from the bottom before she turned from view to climb the second flight to her room.

"No, thanks! The painkillers they gave me made me drowsy. I just want to lie down."

"Oh, ok!" I said, backing down at her rejection. Filled with shame and regret for lashing out at her over broken dishes instead of showing concern for her safety, I stood alone in the kitchen and cried.

Sunbrook Mansion Bed And Breakfast

Guest book comments

"Thank you for the relaxing stay. Great breakfast! I'll call when I'm working in town again."

Chapter 21

The deluge of tears helped me release some of the tension from this morning's accident as well as the stress that had accumulated over my dwindling bank account. The smell of jasmine and the touch of a comforting hand on my shoulder calmed me. My tears stopped, and I raised my head in time to see a red Jaguar speed into the driveway and park. Two handsome young men in polo shirts and jeans emerged from the small, buckskin leather compartment of the expensive car. Panic struck, I rushed to the mirror. Moist, red rimmed eyes stared back at me. "Oh, no, I'm not ready for them yet," I said aloud to the ghost, dabbing the tears with a tissue before grabbing my emergency makeup stash from the drawer. The foundation covered my tear-stained cheeks. Liner and mascara disguise my red eyes. The doorbell didn't ring yet, so I took the extra time to freshen my lipstick and take a couple of deep breaths. At the foyer door, I watched the guests approach, their heads turned east, pointing to the spectacular view of Hollidaysburg, another amenity of Sunbrook.

"Welcome to Sunbrook. I'm your host, Tiffany."

"Hello, Tiffany. I'm Kevin, and this is Tyler."

"Hello," Tyler said without as much as a glance my way. He walked past me into the foyer, then without hesitation into the music room, and then the library. Kevin rolled their luggage to the bottom of the stairs and waited for me to close the door and catch up.

"Let me show you where you'll be having breakfast, before I take you to your room."

Tyler turned his back to me when I approached where he stood with his arms crossed, tapping his foot. My face grew warm and my breathing shallowed. My hands shook, making my fingers fail to hook through the brass pulls of the pocket doors to the dining room. I felt again for the rings and when they released, breathed a silent prayer of thanks for the craftsman who, a century ago, balanced the doors with skillful precision on their hidden tracks. Their massive bulk slid, without effort, through the slot and disappeared into the wall. My fingers fumbled for the light switch. The few seconds it took to find it felt like minutes before the crystal chandelier glistened above.

"What time would you like breakfast served?" I asked, struggling to hold my voice steady.

"We have no idea how late we'll be. I'll let you know tonight, after we return from the wedding. Now take us to our room," Tyler said, leaving the dining area. He climbed the stairs empty handed, ignoring his luggage sitting at the bottom. Before my hand touched the handle, Kevin snatched up both overnight bags when I bent down to pick one up. He carried them with ease, his muscles flexed at their weight. We reached the top where Tyler stood tapping his foot again.

Passing him without looking, I led them to the

Deborah. "The room has a private bath…"

"Well I certainly hope so," Tyler's snide voice interrupted.

"And a balcony," I continued, forcing a smile. "To light the gas fireplace, turn the knob and push the button. My room is at the top of the stairs. Just knock if you need anything."

Tyler walked out of sight into the bathroom. "Ok, thank you! Goodbye," he said, raising his voice.

Kevin's face flushed red. Moisture appeared on his forehead. "It's a lovely room. I'm sure we'll be comfortable. Thank you so much," his kind eyes searched mine for forgiveness.

I answered with a shrug and a reassuring smile, handed him the key, and slipped out closing the door behind me. I forced back tears and resisted the urge to stop at my room and curl up under my covers—the mess in the kitchen came to mind. My feet carried me down the stairs. The defeat that rose from my gut tried to destroy my will, but realizing that with the task at hand, there was no time to feel sorry for myself. Stress sent adrenaline through my veins, cleared my head of self-pity, and ignited me with the energy to clean up the dangerous shards.

"Grace?" Saying her name and my soft knock issued a response, but the thick bedroom door muffled her words. Sure that she had locked me out, I was surprised when the knob turned under my hand, and the door opened. My heart broke at the sight of her mummy-like form lying motionless on the bed. The bandages covering her face and neck, wrapped so close to her eyes, made it difficult to read her mood.

Thank God, the doctor said her eyes escaped injury because of the natural reflex to close them before the flying glass reached her. He also said that her shallow wounds would heal soon, but it was difficult to witness her hour of pain as the nurses, armed with tweezers, pulled out the tiny spears. Each one made a sharp *clink* sound when dropped into stainless, kidney-shaped bowls. Guilt overwhelmed me, my breath quickened, and my body stood ridged ready for her well-deserved wrath.

"What's up?" Her voice sounded unfamiliar with its high meek tone. Not her boisterous, confident speech that told you, *What is up*, in her world anyway, a significant but endearing trait of her personality.

"How ya doin'?" I asked, just above a whisper. My shoulders dropped as the pent up tension released.

"I'm okay. The pain pills finally kicked in, so I was able to sleep."

"Do you want me to get you anything?"

"No, I'm going to get some more shut eye." Her signature tone began to return, giving me some comfort.

"Okay, I'll let you alone for now. The guests staying to attend a wedding have arrived and are all settled in."

"Good to hear. I'm sorry I'm laid up."

"No problem. I can handle a couple of handsome young men while you recoup." My voice remained flippant even when Tyler's behavior entered my mind.

"Young and handsome you say. Well, I might have to pop a couple more of these pain pills."

"You stay put until you're healed. Young and handsome can wait." We both smiled at our jests but soon grew somber.

"I'm sorry I was careless and broke your good china."

"It's alright, Grace! Already forgotten. I'm sorry for the things I said to you. You're a great assistant. Sometimes the pressure gets to me, and I say things I don't mean."

"It's alright, Tiffany! Already forgotten." She grinned then let out a long breath.

"You're tired, I'll let you rest. I'm going to the market to get a few breakfast items. It won't take me long. I'll check on you around suppertime. Maybe your appetite will return by then."

"That would be great, thanks." Her voice had dropped to a whisper. Her lids drooped and then closed. The rhythmic breathing of sleep soon followed.

Guest Book Comments

"Nice vacation from my hectic business trip."

Chapter 22

It didn't take long to put away the groceries. The microwave bell announced that my supper was ready. Pungent herbs and spices mingled with savory tomato sauce wafted from my steaming bowl of spaghetti, leftover from last night's meal. My stomach growled, reminding me that it hadn't been filled since breakfast. Footsteps and voices on the stairs drew my attention. Kevin and Tyler were leaving for the wedding. They were arguing, but from my vantage point only a few words were audible, something about the bride. They kept it up until they closed the door behind them.

***

Grace's appetite had returned, and she gobbled up the vegetable soup. The bowl and spoon now sat on the tray balancing on my arm. Grace added her empty juice glass beside them after she took her pain medication. "Those will knock me out for the night." She huddled under her covers and closed her eyes. My soft-soled shoes helped me to make a quiet exit from the room and a stealthy descent back to the kitchen.

***

With the preparations for breakfast complete, my aching feet trudged back up the stairs. The anticipation of a warm, comforting shower motivated me to reach the top. It's been a long day which won't end until Kevin and Tyler return and tell me what time to serve breakfast.

The shower's soothing water massaged my shoulders and back. The tension of the day dripped from my body, falling at my feet to be carried in a circle down the drain. Calm and bliss enveloped me when the fluffy white bath sheet embraced my body, along with the enchanting walls of Sunbrook—both a cocoon, shielding me from the outside world. Filled with giddy abandon, I grasped the terry corners and began to twirl with outstretched arms. The towel fluttered behind me like butterfly wings. My childish release enlivened my soul until my head grew dizzy and my stomach lurched causing me to stop and sway while the room continued the twirl without me. Then my feet sent me on a precarious stumble to the bed to wait for my nausea and head to clear before donning my nightgown and robe. A touch of makeup was a must to face Kevin and Tyler. Without it, they wouldn't recognize me. Hell, I wouldn't recognize me. I finished with a layer of mascara to my lashes when Mike walked through the door.

"What's with the makeup? You look like you're showered, ready for bed." He stepped into the closet and started to strip.

"I am, but the guests are out, and I have to ask them about breakfast."

"What time will they be back?"

"I don't know."

"So you're going to wait up until they get here. What if it's four in the morning?"

To avoid confrontation, I just shrugged.

"Why do you do this to yourself? You let these people walk all over you. This is your bed and breakfast. Why lose sleep over them? You set the time and if they don't show, they don't eat." Mike talked while he watched me switch on my bedside lamp, get into bed, and open a book. "Whatever," he added with a huff, grabbed his robe and marched in to the bathroom, closing the door between us.

Knowledge of Tyler's rudeness toward me today would have made Mike furious. He may have even waited up with me to confront Tyler. The scenario played through my mind. My face grew hot at the embarrassment it would cause me, so keeping quiet was my only option. Maybe they would return before Mike came out of the bathroom.

He must have rushed through his bedtime ritual tonight because he emerged within the half hour. "What's with the red face? You look as guilty as hell. What are you hiding? Is that a dirty book you're reading?"

"No, I'm just thinking about you." I smiled, holding my ragged breath.

"That's nice! But not tonight, hon! I have to get up an hour early to run for parts." He got into bed, gave me a kiss, and lay down with his back to me. It wasn't long before his shoulder rose and fell with his steady breathing. He was already asleep. It amazed me how easy it was for him to turn his mind off from the stresses of the day.

The bold black letters of "Chapter thirty-four" stared up at me. The Jaguar roared into the driveway.

A car door slammed shut, and another clicked open. A loud argument between Tyler and Kevin ensued across the lot to the portico before being muffled by the roof below our window. The protico door opened, and the argument continued through the foyer and up the stairs. Tyler's loud voice over Kevin's consoling one prompted me to crack the door to listen. When they reached the landing, I stepped out of the comfort of my room, closing the door behind me to protect Mike's sleep. Oh, how I wished of lying sound asleep beside him right now. I watched Tyler slide against the wall up the stairs while Kevin held him steady by the arm.

As soon as they were close, I whispered, "What time would you like breakfast?"

Tyler puffed out his chest and took a step toward me. He hurled obscenities at me in a drunken slur, then raised his voice, and snarled the word "bitch" into my face.

"Shut your trap, Tyler," Kevin hissed. He shoved Tyler ahead of him keeping a stiff hand on the back of his head and neck so that Tyler couldn't turn around. Kevin looked back at me. "Eleven would be good," he whispered then thrust Tyler into their room before softly closing the door behind them.

I backed into my room and, with my quivering hand on the knob, shut the door as quietly as possible. My body quaked, making it a struggle to get into bed. The scene that just happened became a loop running inside my head. My mind tried to make sense of the vicious look in Tyler's eyes and his slur of insults. He had no right or reason to speak to me like that. Anger rose up in my gut, my chest, my throat, its bitterness making me choke. The suffocating heat under the covers forced me to slide off the bed and stumble into the bathroom. I closed the door. My body leaned against its cool wooden bulk, which brought my skin relief from the heat of my anger. The scene returned, replacing anger with pain. The hurt brought sorrow. My hand hit the wall, switching on the light to reveal my reflection in the mirror before me. Wide, sad eyes stared back at me. Tears welled up and ran down my cheeks becoming uncontrollable. I sank to the floor and cried out the pain, muffling my sorrowful sobs with a towel.

***

The bathroom clock's monotonous tick bounced off the tile walls and floor commanding the room. After an hour of lying across its rock-hard surface, the floor assaulted my muscles and bones. My tears were spent, and weakness overwhelmed my body. I positioned myself up on all fours, and the edge of the tub became my point of focus on my way to standing. I crawled to the tub where I pulled myself up to sit, rubbing my knees to ease the pain. My face felt hot. I stood up and looked in the mirror. My eyes were red and puffy. I knew from experience they would give me away at breakfast if I didn't get the swelling down. I refused to give Tyler the satisfaction of knowing he had hurt my feelings. I turned on the faucet and waited until the water ran cold through my fingers, then expected to hear a sizzle when I splashed its icy wetness against the fiery skin of my face.

Guest book comments

"We just had an exceptional B&B experience!"

Chapter 23

Almost ready to go down for breakfast, I watched Mike saunter up behind me in the full length mirror. He slid his arms around my waist and laid his chin on my shoulder. "How about I make us some bacon and eggs before your guests show up for breakfast? What time will that be?"

"Eleven," I said with a quick shrug.

"Wow! That late, huh? They must have come back late last night."

I turned to face him. "You make the best eggs. Let's go down now. I'll make the coffee and toast." I gave him a peck on the lips and backed out of his arms, took his hand, and led him out the door.

The crisp Texas toast's soft center gave way to the knife. The slather of creamy butter melted and dripped down over the thick crust. My mouth watered at the aroma of warm toast melded with sizzling bacon and fresh ground coffee beans. Mike joined me at the table and set a huge dish of sunny-side-up eggs and bacon in front of me. He filled his plate, and we both dug in. We cleaned our plates and enjoyed laughing and talking over steaming mugs of coffee.

"I wish we could spend the whole day together," I said, reaching over the table and entwining my little finger with his.

"Me, too." He gave mine a gentle squeeze. Reluctance washed over Mike's face before he broke our connection and stood. "I gotta go." He lifted his coat from the back of his chair, slid his arms through the quilted sleeves, and flipped it onto his shoulders.

"Come home early tonight," I said, anxious about my day, especially about facing Tyler. "We'll see. Not sure when I'll be home." Slight irritation seeped into his voice and frown lines appeared between his eyes. He must have seen my disappointment because they smoothed away as he pulled me close and wrapped his arms around me. "I'm sorry."

I wanted him to hold me forever. I hated it when we had to part. We've been married twenty-four years, and I still couldn't get enough of him. But life gets in the way because we both had to get to work. "It's ok. I'll see you tonight when you get here."

He held me for a moment more before pulling back, his expression fixed. "I'm gonna be late if I don't get out of here." He kissed my forehead, let go of me, and rushed out the door.

"I love you," I yelled after him. He started his pickup and gave me a palm wave before speeding out of the driveway. I knew I wouldn't get an "I love you" in return. Mike had never said the words but expressed his feelings with actions—like starting my car when it's cold outside, cleaning it off after a snow storm, or keeping an eye on my gas gauge and filling the tank when necessary. Also, brewing the coffee in the morning before I'd come down, or taking notice that I needed more juice for guests and bringing it home on his way from work at night, all without my asking.

The dining room dazzled. Crisp white linens topped with honeysuckle, yellow and white china in an elegant art deco pattern, sparkling crystal goblets, and gleaming silverware all graced the breakfast table. The chandelier glistened overhead, and the stained glass windows threw rich hues of azure and emerald against the walls. Satisfied with the effects, my thoughts turned to the muffin batter that I needed to mix and bake in time for Kevin and Tyler's decent.

Batter dropped into the tin with a mini scoop caused less drips and made the job go faster. Three flavors was a stretch for one person to prepare, but it was important that my guests were pampered regardless of their behavior. With the muffins in the oven, I set out bread and butter for toast, and the ingredients for the vegetable omelets, to have ready to cook. The clock read ten till eleven—time to take the fruit plate, juice, and coffee in to be there for the guests as soon as they were seated. While pulling the pans out of the oven, I heard them coming down the stairs. My breath quickened at the thought of serving Tyler. My hands shook, and the tin wobbled until the muffins almost bounced out of their nests. "Tiffany, pull yourself together! You can do this. Besides, Tyler's the one who should be nervous about facing you," I encouraged myself out loud. My breath slowed and my back straightened; my chest raised and my shoulders shifted back—the result of my positive affirmation. I hoisted up the tray and headed with a determined step to the dining room.

They sat quiet at the table drinking their coffee.

To avoid eye contact with each other, their heads wandered like bobble heads around the room.

"Good morning! I hope you slept well." Not waiting for an answer, I added, "Here are some hot muffins to go with your coffee." I set the heaping china bowl between them. "There are three varieties to choose from—spice, chocolate chip, and apple. In addition, you'll be having ham, cheese, and vegetable omelets, along with whole wheat Texas toast."

"Sounds delicious, and these are tasty, too," Kevin said, after squeezing off a morsel of the chocolate chip flavor.

"I'm glad you like them," I replied.

Tyler selected apple, but he moved in slow motion. He looked like he was hungover or hadn't slept well. I didn't ask which because I didn't care. I pivoted and walked away.

"I'll be back with your eggs and toast as soon as they're ready," I said over my shoulder, not intending to spend any more time with them than necessary.

***

Their voices and footsteps climbing the stairs announced that they were finished with breakfast. After cleaning up and washing the delicate dishes by hand, the idea of rest with my feet up in my favorite plush velvet chair enticed me. The afternoon sun's rays streamed through the library's tall window radiating its warmth over my body. With eyes closed, my face rose seeking to absorb its natural renewed vitality. A slight click pulled me from my reverie. I opened my eyes to see Tyler standing in front of my display of family photographs on a table beside the fireplace. He held one of the frames, staring at the picture, his brow furrowed. Startled by his presence, my quick involuntary intake of breath caused him to jump and almost drop the photo.

"Oh, I'm sorry to disturb you. I didn't see you sitting there." He looked at me and set the frame back in its original spot as he spoke, but then dropped his eyes and clasped his hands behind his back.

"I didn't hear you come in." I fought to recall the obnoxious, hostile bastard of yesterday while the warmth of compassion welled up in my chest as he stood still in silence, like a child caught in the act. "It's alright. These rooms are for guests to enjoy, too." He remained in place. "You're welcome to look around."

"Thank you," he said ready to say something else but was interrupted by the sound of someone descending the stairs. We both looked into the foyer to see Kevin bound down the last couple of steps and strut through the door to stand beside Tyler.

"I'm ready to go if you are," he said and then smiled when he noticed me. "Oh, Tiffany, we'll be out until this evening, but we won't be late tonight. We'll be shoving off early tomorrow. Would it be alright to have breakfast at seven?"

"Of course! I hope you like French toast."

"Sounds good to me! You like it too, don't you, Tyler?"

"Yes," he answered and picked up the photo he was holding a minute ago. "Who are the men in this picture?" He turned it toward me.

"That's my cousin, Terrance, and his husband

Charles. I took that last year, a couple of days before their wedding in Napa Valley, California."

"Oh," Tyler's eyes were wide with surprise. "I owe you an apology for my behavior yesterday. I misunderstood when I called to make the reservations and you wanted to book us separate rooms. I was offended because I thought you were in disagreement of our lifestyle. I wanted to cancel our stay, but Kevin refused and insisted we could handle it. He was a perfect gentleman, but I acted like a first class jerk. Will you please forgive me?"

"I always verify how many rooms, to be sure… anytime I take a reservation. I'm known to be thorough, sometimes too thorough. My assistant, Grace, reminds me of that often. You'll be meeting her tomorrow. She's a hoot. Yes, I accept your apology and nothing more needs to be said about it. You have a good day, and I'll see you at seven in the morning. Take care."

They left. Kevin on a cheerful note with Tyler following behind sporting an apprehensive smile, but with his shoulders relaxed in relief.

Guest book comments

"Thank you for the enjoyable stay. We enjoyed all the nooks and crannies! Thank you for letting us explore them."

Chapter 24

The sound of footsteps overhead pulled me to the bottom of the stairs where Grace came into view. She descended with slow, sure steps as she held onto the railing with both hands. Her face scrunched up in pain at each movement. She stopped and sniffed the air as the scent of jasmine filled the foyer. She rolled her eyes and then continued to totter down the last few steps.

"Are you sure you should be out of bed?" I asked. "You still look sore."

"Yeah, and I'd be sore in more ways than one if I didn't get out of that damn room. That lyin' around is tiresome. I need to limber up and get to work. Besides, I'm starved." She made her way into the kitchen, pulled a package of bacon and a carton of eggs out of the fridge, and set them on the counter. She bent down and grabbed a skillet out of the cupboard below the stove. My hand reached out to help her up but stopped midair when she motioned for me to get back. "Stop hovering and go find something to do. It's a big house. I'm sure something, somewhere, needs your attention."

"Ok, I'll leave you alone, but if you need help, I'll be in my office."

"And take your ghost with you," Grace yelled after me.

I slapped a hand over my mouth to suppress a laugh. The ghost's giggle echoed through the rooms.

"Oh, brother," Grace grumbled.

I chuckled as I plopped down at my desk. A pulse thumped at my temples when my eyes settled on the bills piled at center stage before me. I picked them up and flipped through them.

The amount due assaulted me and killed my good mood. "Can't put this off any longer," I told myself, so I squared my shoulders and grabbed the pen and checkbook from the top drawer.

With a sigh, I finished writing the last checks. I studied the balance in the checkbook, and a panic attack began to build. "What will we do if another major repair hits?" Jasmine wafted around me, and inspiration struck. *I'll step up my advertising for weddings and more parties.* I caught another wave of delicious aroma, and within minutes of placing the ads, I felt calm. To treat myself for finishing these tasks, I decided to explore the house's nooks and crannies.

"Grace! I'm going up to refresh the guest rooms, then to the third floor."

"Don't do the rooms. I will."

I opened my mouth, a debate ready to roll off my tongue.

"And don't argue with me either!" she added.

My lips snapped shut, and then I dashed up the stairs.

The flight to the third floor taxed my lungs. My feet became lead weights—my muscles strained to lift them onto the top step. I collapsed onto the pine floor. A long, narrow hall stretched before me. Curiosity gripped me when I spied the small door at the other end, prompting me to force my body to get up. I wondered where the door would lead me. *Maybe today is the time to finally check out this part of our mansion,* I thought. My legs wobbled at first, but moving each foot forward helped them to recover. Half way down the hall, the mellow light of the winter sun cast its rays through the thick glass of the skylight. I paused, and with eyes closed, raised my face to bask in the warm glow—one of Sunbrook's gifts, a fleeting moment of bliss with God's creation.

The wing knob on the cubby door turned without resistance, and the flip-latch lifted. The door stuck at first, but with a second tug, it opened. Jasmine permeated from the opening overwhelming my senses. I fanned my hand in front of my face. "I'm glad you're with me, but could you tone down on the aroma? It's a bit much," I said to the ghost.

"Here," she said.

"Believe me, there is no question you're here."

"Here," the voice spoke again.

"I am here," I said, searching the darkness. The light from the hall caught a long string hanging from a four-foot ceiling. I grasped it tight and pulled. A dull shine from a bare incandescent bulb filled a four-by-five-foot space, but its light didn't reach through to the dark void beyond. The small area was empty except for a green child's chair against the wall on the right. It appeared to have been crafted from an old wooden fruit crate. *A time-out chair? Why would that be the only thing in* here? I wondered. Looking around, I couldn't imagine anyone locking a child in here for punishment, but there was no way to open the door from the inside. It had no knob. A flat brass plate was the only hardware. My mind raced with thoughts of a frightened child screaming and crying desperate to get out. *Get hold of yourself, Tiffany. The Lloyds wouldn't do that. They had a sterling reputation.*

I peered into the dark void and scanned the walls for a light switch but found nothing. I raced down the hall and snatched the flashlight from its charger, then scurried back, and crawled past the sad little chair. I pointed the flashlight into the blackness and pressed the button.

Guest book comments

"Thank you! We really enjoyed the quiet atmosphere and the history of Sunbrook."

Chapter 25

I crawled a short distance before the ceiling rose to eight feet. I stood and rubbed my smarting knees. The flashlight's wide beam reached a wall about twenty-five feet away. My hand held the light steady as I pivoted to the right and discovered twenty-five feet the other way. The square room held three cardboard boxes stacked in one corner. Four brown suitcases stood against the far wall. All were draped in spider webs. On closer inspection, the suitcases were covered with the entwined letters "LV", the initials of a famous designer. *Wow, why would anybody leave these behind? They're worth a small fortune.* I laid the biggest on its side. "Let's hope they hold a large fortune," I said aloud and flipped open the two brass latches. The lid lifted without resistance to reveal John Lloyd's bank statements, canceled checks, and several ledgers. After rustling through them, I pulled the next case down on its side and opened it. It held more of the same. I'd check them later. Maybe something exciting is hiding among the mogul's financial papers. My fingers fumbled with the latches on the smaller case. It contained even more ledgers and statements.

The last one, a toiletries train case, held old books, all leather bound with pages edged in gold. I picked through works by Thoreau, Emerson, and

Melville, and marveled at their great condition. They had survived years in hibernation during hot summers and freezing winters. I placed the books back into their archives, then closed and latched the lid, checking to make sure it sealed again. "I'll take these down to the library."

After placing the case near the entrance, I returned to the cardboard boxes, and with one hand, tugged open the flaps of the first box. I aimed the flashlight at its contents. On top lay a large book with the word *Journal* printed in three inch letters across the cover. Not sure if the boxes had protected it as well as the suitcases, I gently lifted the hard cover—it proved to be in good shape. The first page was blank but the next one had "John Lloyd's" name written in the thick script of a fountain pen with the year 1875 below. The paper stayed intact when I leafed through the pages filled with more of the same black script. I pulled out the book to reveal another. The box held at least six of John Lloyd's journals. The next two boxes also contained a treasure trove of writings in his hand. *These must go downstairs,* I decided, *but there are too many to carry along with the books. One would do for now.* I grabbed the top journal and headed for the hall, holding it tight against my body. The flashlight wobbled as my other hand grasped the handle of the train case.

"Wait! Here."

My feet stopped mid-step, stuck to the floor. I twisted at the waist and fanned the light around the dark space. A faint white mist swirled within the beam in the center of the room and then disappeared.

My body trembled. Air stuck in my lungs. Sweat bled through my skin as my adrenaline rose. The ghost had never materialized before, and for the first time she frightened me. My mind willed my foot to step backwards.

"Wait! Here." This time the voice came from the other end of the room. She moved further away, so I stopped and stood waiting for her next command. Silence filled the room, and after a few more minutes my awkward stance caused my calf to cramp. The pain became unbearable, so I lifted my toes to stretch it out.

"Wait! Here."

Her voice became muffled. *Had she moved to the next room*, I wondered. *Escape from the creepy darkness*, filled my thoughts.

"I can't wait here. I've got to get out," I said.

Still clutching the journal and case, my body turned and limped toward the small entrance. I bent over where the ceiling lowered, put one knee on the floor, and stopped dead. The door had closed. Panic struck, I dropped the flashlight. It clattered onto the floor and went out. Now in darkness, I struggled to breathe and flailed out my arms in front of me. Claustrophobia overwhelmed me until my eyes adjusted to the dark. I then spied a crack through the doorway where a sliver of light glowed from the hallway. "Thank God, the door hadn't latched!" I released the air from my lungs. The flashlight blinked to life on the floor in front of me. I grabbed and shook it until the light steadied; then, pointed it at the door. My breath caught in my throat when the beam exposed a multitude of scratch marks made by tiny fingers desperate to get out.

Guest book comments

"Sunbrook B&B is a lovely place to spend restful time."

Chapter 26

My back leaned tight against my bedroom door where I paused to catch my breath and try to comprehend what I'd just witnessed. My head shook as if it could erase the scene of the ghost's mist and her voice commanding me to stay in the darkness with her. Fear had never clutched my chest so tight. It made me frantic to escape the dark confines before I became trapped. The scratches in the old varnish of the small door were proof that someone had been trapped long ago. The little chair convinced me that children were locked in there. What other secrets were hidden within Sunbrook Mansion's walls? What other ghosts inhabited Sunbrook Mansion's nooks and crannies, waiting for the chance to make themselves known? Someone from Sunbrook's past had forced little children into that cramped space—a large hand against their tiny chest, shoving them back as they struggled to get out, taking a moment to enjoy the terror in the child's eyes before slamming the door. A cruel smile of satisfaction appeared on the face, as the fingers turned the latch, relishing in the power to decide when the child will be freed. A shiver rocked my body at the vivid scene I'd conjured and at the thought of the possibility of an encounter with this evil specter. The weight of the case of books brought me from my self-induced trance. My hand cramped around the handle causing my numb fingers to loosen their grip. Now the case dangled by the tips. I set it on the floor beside the bed and bent down to shove it underneath then slid the journal close beside it. I sat on the floor against the bed and held out my shaking hands then hugged my quivering stomach.

"Tiffany, are you there?" Grace asked through the door. Startled, my throat tightened and blocked my attempt to answer. She knocked softly. "Tiffany."

I forced myself up, sat on the bed and cleared my throat. "Yes," I managed to say with a somewhat steady voice.

"You're wanted on the telephone. It's Sharon, you know, that crazy woman who's having the party this weekend." I sat silent, trying to comprehend. "I can tell her to call back. She'll probably spaz out, but it would be my pleasure to shut her down."

Her words brought me back to reality. "No don't. I'm coming." My hand gripped the bed's foot rail when I stood struggling for balance. My feet moved toward the door where Grace was still talking. "Alright, I'll go tell her to hold her horses."

"Just tell her that I'm coming, Grace," I said, in a stern voice, flustered. I crossed the room and jerked open the door.

"Ok, ok," she said with her hands up in retreat and then bolted down the steps ahead of me. "Miss Sharon, m'lady will be with you pronto." I heard Grace say in a syrupy southern drawl as I stepped onto the landing. My feet churned down the rest of the stairs to where Grace stood holding the receiver out from her ear away from Sharon's shrieks.

"Whatever," Grace growled into the mouthpiece, then dropped it onto my pile of paid bills and sashayed to the kitchen.

I leaped forward and grasped the phone shoving it to my ear. "Hello Sharon, this is Tiffany. I'm sorr…"

"Well, it's about time and you better be sorry. Does the bitch that answered the phone work for you?" Not giving me a chance to answer, she continued. "Fire her! I don't want her working at my party. She's obnoxious and rude."

"*Look who's talking*," I silently mouthed into the phone. "I have everything ready for your party," I said, ignoring her comments. "The ambiance of the lit candles in the fireplaces will be stunning…"

"I'll decide that myself when I see them. My friend…"

"*You have a friend?"* I mouthed again.

"…Jeffry is dropping off a case of liquor Saturday afternoon. I don't want it stolen. You be there, so he can bring it inside. Don't touch it. I'll set up the bar when I get there. That's all for now." *Click.*

My face grew hot, and I shook the phone, strangling it with both hands, pretending it was Sharon's neck. Putting up with the hostess from hell will destroy my anxiety coping skills. I'll be in a strait jacket before the night's over. Grace will be in handcuffs! *Thank heavens she will be at the Lancaster outlets!*

Guest book comments

Sunbrook is a charming B&B. We will be back!"

Chapter 27

Tyler and Kevin were checking out after breakfast. We've been cordial since yesterday once I cleared up Tyler's misunderstanding toward me, so serving them would be stress free. The scent of cinnamon and fresh baked French toast warming in the oven permeated the rooms. Overcome by calm, while resigned to its allure, I sighed, leaned back in my chair, closed my eyes and inhaled the sweet aroma.

"Whatcha doing? Sleeping on the job?"

I jumped, and my eyes flew open. Every nerve stood at attention, and it took a couple of seconds for my senses to evaluate the situation. Grace stood near me, bent over, staring with her face only a few inches from mine, her lips sporting an amused smirk.

"What the hell, Grace?" I leaned away from her, my hand over my heart. Voices and footsteps on the stairs alerted me to Tyler and Kevin's descent. "Get away from me." I shoved her aside to get to the fridge, pulled out a pack of sausage and turned on the griddle. She walked over to the counter beside me and lobbed her arm around my shoulders.

"Sorry, old girl. I thought it would be funny to scare you. At least I didn't yell 'boo.' I almost did, ya know. Thought better of it though when I saw you so relaxed. Feared you might fall off the chair, even if it would have been comical to watch," she said while jerking me against her at almost every word.

"Would you get off me?" I pushed her away. "What's wrong with you this morning? Did you take too many pain pills? Are you high?"

"Nah, but I did take one oxy. This is the first day I've felt good since I acted stupid, broke the good china, and became a pin cushion." She moved around the island to the oven and opened the door. She picked up the potholders, pulled out the French toast, and set it on the counter. Then leaning forward with her hands placed flat on each side of the hot dish, she looked at the floor, paused as if in thought, and then looked back up at me, her eyes serious. "Listen, I'm sorry. I was acting stupid again. I promise never to scare you like that in the future. Please, forgive me."

Still a little peeved, I placed three sausage links on a plate and then slid it over to Grace. "Alright, I forgive you. Now let's get these plates filled, so I can serve Tyler and Kevin. They said their plan was to check out and get on the road early."

After gathering up the dishes from the dining room, I untied my apron and threw it over the kitchen chair. "Listen Grace, I'm going to work at 2nd Hand Rose today. You clean the bedrooms and all of downstairs rooms, so they're ready for Sharon's party. Do a good job because I'm sure her evil eyes will be searching for something to complain about."

"Are there any guests booked for the two days before the party?"

I headed for the door. "No," I said without

looking back.

Gwen and I stayed late to price consignment items and rolled them out on the sales floor, hanging each piece of clothing in its correct size on the rack. Then we arranged accessories, such as handbags, hats, and jewelry in several vignettes to entice shoppers to purchase to complete their outfits. It took us an hour to finish the displays before we said goodnight.

After stopping for pizza on the way home, I floated my big ol' Cadillac into the garage at eight forty-five. The spotless kitchen caught my eye when I paused to set my supper on the counter. *Nice job, Grace. I'll keep you on despite the trick you pulled this morning.* Then with my hand on the railing, I pulled myself up the stairs anticipating the hot, soothing shower waiting at the top.

***

Dressed in my pajamas and feeling refreshed from a shower, I bounced down the stairs to heat the pizza and get back to my room, hoping to avoid Grace on the way. She would have to wait until tomorrow for us to be pals again.

Guest book comments

"Tiffany, you are so warm and welcoming. We look forward to staying in the future."

Chapter 28

My next guests arrived after supper. The local Snaps gym hired a girl from Hooters to appear at a special promotion to attract new members. Steve, the owner, had booked two rooms for tonight, one for Angela, the girl from Hooters, and one for her bodyguard, Hunter. I watched them drive up while folding towels in the laundry room. I left the portico door unlocked, so I didn't rush to meet them. I folded the last towel then carried the basket with me to the foyer. A beautiful petite girl, about nineteen years old, met me. "Hi, I'm Angela. I love this place. It's so big. I never dreamed I would be staying in a mansion. How cool is this?" she said, staring up at the oak coffered ceilings and stained glass windows above the staircase landing.

"Hello. I'm Tiffany. Welcome to Sunbrook, Angela." Hunter, her burly bodyguard, followed with his thick muscles flexed, carrying their overnight bags. Charles Atlas came to mind.

Steve, another Atlas, filled the doorway. "Hey listen, you two! I gotta get back to the gym. I'll pick you up tomorrow at 11:00. Be ready! We have to be in Atlantic City by 6:00." Then he rushed out the door. Hunter looked after Steve like he longed to follow him, then looked all around, a bit apprehensive. I wasn't sure what was wrong until he looked at me and with a slight edge in his voice said, "Do you live here?"

"Yes."

"Aren't you scared? I didn't want to stay when we pulled up, but Steve insisted—wouldn't budge. This big old house gives me the creeps."

"I love it," Angela chimed in.

I couldn't believe the contrast of the two. She's tiny and sweet, delighted at the chance to stay here. He's big and strong but dreaded staying the night. "Follow me, I'll show you where you'll be having breakfast." I walked through the library and into the dining room.

"Wow, this is beautiful," Angela said, stepping into the room. Hunter and I watched as she put her arms out and twirled the length of the room with dramatic flair, then sat on the window seat, and gazed out. She looked so beautiful, and I was amused by her youthful enthusiasm.

"Yah, this is great," Hunter said. Angela's performance distracted him and his shoulders relaxed like they were relieved of an invisible weight.

"I'll show you to your rooms now."

Angela turned and jumped up from the window seat. She reached out to touch the mahogany dining table where she let her hand linger before she swept it across the ornate chair backs as she walked through the room. She came to an abrupt stop in the library. "Wait. Tell us about the house."

"Okay," I said and proceeded to go through my mental list of the history and important points about the house.

"Is there a ghost?" she asked smiling and holding her body tense with her hands clutched in front of her as if praying that there was.

I hesitated, not sure if I should reveal Sunbrook's specter. But Angela's stance prompted me to fulfill her imagination. "Yes, there is a ghost."

She squealed with glee. "Tell us some stories about it." I told her about Jack, the Dupont guest, and his missing socks. "Tell us another one." Her eyes stared wide with anticipation and her hands were still clutched in prayer begging for more.

"No, please don't tell us anymore ghost stories. I don't want to hear anymore. I won't be able to sleep tonight." Hunter startled me with his abrupt outburst and left me speechless. I would have thought he was joking but this herculean man, beneath his thick bearded face, possessed the stare of a frightened child. Hunter was standing behind Angela so she couldn't see his petrified look. She either was oblivious to his fear or she just didn't care because she whined, "But I want to hear more."

"Maybe later! Let me show you the music room," I said trying to distract Angela away from ghosts. "I call it the music room because of the antique pump organ and the musical theme throughout. I pointed to the fan shaped fireplace screen embossed with brass musical notes and then to the picture of angels descending Jacob's ladder while playing trumpets. "It would have originally been the parlor where the Lloyds would receive guests and gather for family activities."

"Cool," Angela said.

"You're welcome to use these rooms down here or you can explore the third floor maid's quarters."

"You mean… you have maids," Angela said with a look of awe.

"I wish. No, they're long gone, but the rooms are untouched."

They followed me up the stairs. I took Angela to her room first. "This is actually the bridal chamber. I thought you might like the canopy bed."

"Yes, I like it very much." She wandered slowly to the bed, taking in everything, as if bewitched. Hunter set her overnight bag on the luggage stand.

"Hunter, your room is across the vestibule from here. "You're in the Carrie Ann room. It has a TV. I thought you might want to watch."

"Okay, thanks." He walked into the room and set his bag down looking around. Angela bounded through the door. "What's your room look like? Nice." She said stretching the word "ni-i-ce", head bobbing.

"Angela, will you come in and watch television with me?"

I stepped out and walked to the top of the steps.

"Sure, as soon as I get my pajamas on."

"Okay, but hurry. I don't want to be alone." I heard him say as I descended the stairs to the kitchen. I set the table for breakfast, sliced fruit, and programmed the coffee pot. It was after 11:00 when I started up to bed. At my bedroom door, I noticed Hunter's door was still open and heard him say to Angela, "Please stay and watch TV with me just a little longer."

"No. I'm getting sleepy. I'm going to bed. If you're scared, leave on the light and the TV while you fall asleep. I can't stay up any longer." I could see Angela standing in the doorway, looking adorable in her yellow flannel pajamas and matching slippers. "Keep your door open.

"Will you keep yours open, too?"

"No! Goodnight," she said.

I closed my door and listened to the pat of her fluffy slippers on the parquet floor as she crossed to her own room; then, her door clicked shut.

I decided to keep the hall light on for Hunter's reassurance. I showered, dressed, and settled into bed. The *Tonight Show* theme was playing as I dozed off.

***

Morning broke early, but I managed to make it to the kitchen by 6:30. I had everything prepared when I heard Hunter and Angela on the stairs at 9:00. I picked up the tray, smiled and gave a cheerful "good morning" as I bustled into the dining room with a bounty of fresh blueberry muffins, fruit art, juice, and coffee. "I hope you both slept well."

Angela sat at the table. "I had a long, peaceful sleep. My room was so cozy and quiet. I had a calming bath this morning and as I lay there, relaxed with my eyes closed, the sunshine burst through the window, covering my body. It was great. I was tanning in the tub!"

"Sounds heavenly! I'm glad you enjoyed it, Angela," I said, longing for the experience.

Hunter poured the coffee and reached for a

muffin. He popped a piece in his mouth. "I slept a couple of hours." His words were somewhat muffled as he chewed. "I was watching TV, and at about 3:00 a.m. the screen went black. It shut off all by itself. I was afraid to move, but I slowly settled down under the covers and tried to go to sleep. I lay there for about fifteen minutes when I felt a hard pressure on my chest. I froze, but then it pressed even harder, so I jumped up and switched on the light. The room was empty. It scared the hell out of me. I ran over and knocked on your door, Angela, but you didn't wake up, so I crept back to my room and sat up in bed with the light on. I must have finally dozed off and slept until the alarm woke me this morning."

"Wow, Hunter. Did that really happen?" Angela's brow furrowed, and she gave him a sideways look of disbelief.

"Yes, Angela. It really happened." He glared at her, his body stiff and muscles tense as if ready for a fight.

"Okay, okay. I believe you." She leaned back with both palms up, warding off his challenge.

"I'm sorry you encountered such a traumatic ordeal," I interrupted, acting as referee to calm him down. "I believe you. Your night is really not that unusual for Sunbrook."

"Well, I have to tell you, I'm glad I'm not staying another night, ever." That said, he stuffed half of a muffin into his mouth, barely chewing, before he swallowed and gulped down his coffee.

I grappled for an exit line. "Enjoy your fruit, and I'll be right back with your banana pancakes and sausage."

"Mmmm, sounds good." I heard Angela muse as I retreated to the kitchen.

After breakfast Hunter was slouched in his chair, his right leg straight out, looking relaxed. "Today's paper is in the library if you would like to catch up on the news while you're waiting for Steve to pick you up.

"No thanks! I'm waiting outside."

"Maybe you would like to walk the grounds and check out the playhouse."

Angela jumped up and said, "Oh, I want to do that. Walk with me, Hunter."

Hunter mumbled something about being tired but got up and followed her out onto the porch. I watched them follow the path to the playhouse and then began cleaning up. I just finished when Steve pulled up under the portico. I dropped my dish towel onto the counter and went to meet him in the foyer. "Hi Steve, Hunter and Angela are on the front porch." I opened the door, and we walked out onto the porch.

"Okay, guys, the bags are in the car. It's time to get on the road if we're going to make Atlantic City by 6:00.

"I'm ready," Hunter said and started for the car.

"Hunter's a little spooked about this place," Steve said.

"I really liked it here! Thanks," Angela favored me with a little wave then disappeared around the corner.

"Thanks," Steve said. "I'll be booking more rooms. I'm having another promotion in a couple of weeks."

"Great, give me a call."

"There will be four guests next time, and I'm pretty sure Hunter won't be one of them."

"I'm not surprised."

"Thanks again," he said, then turned, and rushed around the corner out of sight.

I wandered back inside realizing that I was all alone and had a couple of hours to myself before the next guests arrived. I looked up and saw the sunlight resonating through the stained glass windows on the staircase and smiled. Then, without hesitation I vaulted up the stairs to work on my tan.

Guest book comments

"Sunbrook is a beautiful place. We definitely will tell my friends and family."

Chapter 29

I gazed out the bedroom window to a sea of white. Large snowflakes hurried to add to the thick cotton-like blanket covering the landscape. Our view of Hollidaysburg had vanished behind the frosty curtain. The tree limbs and bushes plumped up three times their size. Bowed to submission, their black skeletal undersides peeked out from under the onslaught, and I imagined them praying for mercy. The snowflakes were the only thing in motion. I began to pray for mercy. If this storm lasted beyond today, the roads would be a slippery-slide to Sharon's party, especially up the hill of Sunbrook's narrow driveway. I turned toward the bed and found Mike's heavenly blue eyes on me. My heart skipped, and desire wiped the worry of weather and Saturday's party from my mind. I hurried to pull my pajama t-shirt over my head and slid down the pants to step out of them. Then leaped for the bed and snuggled into the circle of Mike's arms.

***

The phone on the bedside table tweeted a few times before Mike answered it. Through a blanket of sleep I heard him agree with his father that he should stay home today. The joy of it brought me fully awake, and I leaned up, resting on my elbow to look into his face.

"You mean, it's not Sunday, and we'll be together the whole day?" I asked, thrilled at the expectation of spending another day with him this week.

"Yes, won't it be fu-u-u-n." With a mischievous smile, he tickled my middle making me squiggle and giggle until I begged him to stop. He rolled over and hopped out of bed, "We thoroughly enjoyed the bed, Tiffany, now let's have breakfast, like the sign out front says." He reached under the covers and tickled me again before heading for the bathroom. "I'll get the shower going." He turned back to look at me. His "get lost in the moment" blue eyes sparkled. He jerked his head once toward the door, "Join me?"

***

"The toast is ready," I said, sliding my arms around Mike's waist and laying my cheek against his back as he flipped the eggs. Filled with contentment, I wanted to cling to him for the rest of our unexpected, precious day together.

"Wowee! It sure smells good in here." We heard Grace say before she appeared and stood at the kitchen entrance. "Am I interrupting or can I join you for breakfast?" Without waiting for an answer, she strolled in, leaned over the griddle, and inhaled the aroma of the sizzling bacon.

I dropped my arms from around Mike's waist. "Good morning, Grace," I sighed, picked up the plate of buttered toast, and carried it to the table.

"Sure, Grace. You're not interrupting anything," Mike said. "Here, you take these eggs, and I'll whip up two more for myself." He scooped the eggs onto a plate and added a couple of pieces of bacon.

I sat, and Grace took the chair across from me. To avoid eye contact, I stared out the breakfast nook's bay window at the panoramic view of the new fallen snow. Grace grabbed some toast and dipped into her eggs. She didn't seem to notice I resented her presence, but deep down I felt glad. I've learned that holding grudges serves little purpose and only ends in regret and hurt feelings. My resolve began to soften just thinking about it. Mike set my plate before me and joined us at the head of the table.

"The snow's letting up," Mike said between mouthfuls. "See," he pointed his fork toward the window, "the sky is clear on the horizon. I'll shovel the sidewalks after breakfast."

I watched him eat and smiled, thinking that our morning frolic is what gave him his hearty appetite.

We finished eating, then lounged over our coffee, and talked. Grace took her last gulp and stood. "I'll clean up." She stacked the dishes on her arm; she stuck her fingers in the empty mugs, gripping all three at once, and put them in the sink.

Mike reached over and took my hand in his, brought it to his lips, and placed a gentle kiss on my fingers. My lips parted, and my breath caught at his uncharacteristic display of affection. He winked and stood pulling me up with him. "See ya later, Grace," he said, leading me from the room.

"Oh brother," we heard Grace groan before we scurried up the stairs.

***

"Where're my snow boots? They're not here," I heard Mike's muffled voice from inside the closet.

I strained to pull up my jeans, jumping to get the waistband over my hips.

"They're in the mud room closet downstairs." I struggled with the snap and zipper. *These must have shrunk in the dryer.*

Mike came out of the closet in his stocking feet equipped with his winter hat, coat, scarf, and gloves. "Okay, I'm ready to tackle the elements." He looked down at his feet and wiggled his toes, "As soon as I cover these puppies," he said, mimicking a child's voice.

I laughed so hard my jeans snap popped, and the zipper trailed down. "Do you think you can find your boots on your own?" I did a couple of deep knee bends and the zipper and snap closed without a fight. "I'll be out in a little while. I have a few things to tidy up around here." My hand waved toward all the bedrooms.

"You don't have to come out at all. Besides, we only have one shovel. I'm sure I can handle it on my own." He bent his arm up to display his muscle then changed into various body builder poses. I burst out laughing—my snap popped, and my zipper trailed down again.

After changing into a pair of stretch slacks, I started cleaning, eager to finish and join Mike. The consistent scrape of the shovel across the cement walk as background noise calmed me enough to keep up my momentum. The full length mirror in the vestibule, my last task, began to sparkle as my cotton cloth moved across the smooth surface. I stopped to focus on my reflection and reality stared back at me. I had been in denial. My jeans didn't shrink. My waist, hips, and thighs all looked thicker. I realized that I had used food to ease my concerns about the mansion's budget woes. Studying my body, I decided right then that these extra pounds had to go. Mike's loud and crisp whistle resonated from outside, interrupting my pep talk. I jogged to the window and looked out to see him standing beside a four-foot tall letter "k" shoveled into the snow. He fanned out his arm in presentation and bowed. My eyes scanned the visage below and then filled with tears. My heart wanted to burst when I read the word "Sunbrook" carved across the driveway. I laid my hands on my chest and let out a sigh of bliss. Mike isn't the romantic kind of guy, but his snow etching showed me that he understood how much Sunbrook meant to me. He leaned on his shovel looking up, awaiting my response. I swiped tears from my cheeks, applauded, and blew a kiss to my hero.

Guest book comments

"Sunbrook has made our first night as husband and wife memorable."

Chapter 30

"Michael did an excellent job plowing and salting the driveway. It's almost bare, so the guests attending Sharon's party shouldn't have any trouble driving up tonight," I said. Thank heavens our son, Michael, wiped out my slippery-slide scenario.

"His new Boss plow is monstrous, like his truck, and he knows how to handle it. I'm proud at how skilled he is at his job, and I had very little to do with it, he taught himself," Mike replied.

Michael, our only child, to our surprise had tested gifted during grade school. We should have known because he had an insatiable curiosity through the years. We had chastised him when he dismantled his mechanical toys and later his computer. He studied their intricate parts and then reassembled them to work again.

"I better get to work. Do you need any more tables set up before I go?"

"No, in fact, you have been most helpful fulfilling all my needs these past two days." I batted my eyes and moved in close for my goodbye kiss. "You're my hero, remember?"

"Yeah, right," he said, smiling. Then his full lips parted, his pupils dilated, and I drowned in the high tide of those ocean-blue eyes. As they pulled me in deep, his arm hooked around my waist and squeezed me against him. “It was my pleasure,” he whispered before his mouth pressed onto mine in a lingering kiss. He released me, leaving me to wobble until I grasped the back of the chair to steady myself. My eyes never left him until his truck pulled out of the driveway. Then, my hand covered my heart where I held our treasured moments of the last two days.

“Oh good, I missed the ‘farewell’,” Grace scoffed from behind me as she walked into the kitchen. “I’ve had enough of walking in on the lovey-dovey stuff after a couple of days being snowbound with you two.”

I rolled my eyes and then turned to face her. “What time are you leaving for the outlets?”

“Because of the weather, there’s been change in plans. Mom and my sister, Julie, are picking me up at five-thirty. We’re going to supper and then to a movie. “What time is devil woman slithering in?”

“It’s none of your business, Grace. Have fun! And I don’t want to see you back here before sunrise tomorrow.”

“No problem.” She poured herself a cup of coffee. “Are you sure you and Gwen can handle it alone? You both are pretty nice, you know. The nicer you are to her, the more evil she gets. One kind move, and she might attack you with her pitch fork.”
Grace took a sip of coffee. My eyes met hers over the cup. Her mouth sprayed coffee across the floor as we both bent over in convulsive laughter. Gwen parked her car and waved at me through the window as she approached the door. She hopped aside when Grace almost collided with her while barrowling

through to her sister's car.

"Sorry Gwen, I'm making my escape before it's too late. God help you both because you'll need it," she yelled before sliding into the back seat. Her arm waved out the window until the car disappeared from view.

"What did she mean by that?" Gwen asked.

"Oh nothing, except the hostess of the party can be a bit difficult sometimes, but I'm sure we can handle her." I reached toward her. "Here, let me take your coat. Have a seat. I made us some tea." I directed her to a chair in the breakfast nook. "Thanks for coming early to help me with the finishing touches. Sharon should be here at six."

"Oh, I forgot, it's *the* Sharon," Gwen said. "Now I understand Grace's comment."

"She is bringing all the food, drink and dishware. All we have to do is put on the tablecloths and arrange the flowers Sharon's florist delivered earlier. I already placed the candles and they are going to look beautiful when lit. She may want us to light them but don't worry—when she decides, she'll let us know."

We had everything ready and sat back down at the table to pour more tea when Sharon's car pulled into the driveway. She and three other women stepped out. Sharon raised the trunk, and they gathered around for her to fill up their arms with baskets and boxes containing assorted party foods and supplies. Weighed down by their load, they paraded behind Sharon through the portico door. She started barking orders in the foyer, and we heard the tap of heels rushing to and fro following each command.

"Do you want to play rummy?" I asked Gwen, hoping to distract her from listening to Sharon's rudeness toward her helpers. "I have the cards right here." I reached across the table, picked them up, and started shuffling.

"What?" She drew her attention from Sharon's bellowing across the other rooms and looked down at the cards. "Oh…yeah… I'll play." She picked up the cards I dealt her and fanned them out in front of her face, her elbows on the table. "What time does the party start?"

"The guests should be arriving around seven." I picked up a card and laid down a discard.

Gwen picked up my discard. "I hope for their sake no one's late or I'll bet they'll hear the wrath of that one in there." She laid down three kings and discarded. Her eyes never left her fan of cards.

We played three games and about to start the fourth when Sharon marched in and stood over us. We both looked up, elbows on the table, hands holding up our fan of cards before us. She crossed her arms in front, and the toe of her shoe tapped the Georgia pine in double time. Her beady green eyes glared down at me.

"I need the candles lit…now," she growled. Then, without waiting for a reply, she spun on her heels and marched back to the foyer.

"What the hell was that?" Gwen asked. Her brow creased. "Why was she so rude to you?"

"Oh, she always acts like that. This game will have to wait." I laid down my cards and stood. "Do you want to help me? It's the last job I'm doing for her tonight. After that she's on her own, and we can get back to our game."

"Sure." Gwen followed me to the music room. I peeked in first, hoping to avoid Sharon as we went about our task. We didn't need her over our shoulder giving orders on how to light candles. "All clear," I motioned for Gwen to follow.

We had the candles in the fireplace and around the room lit and started for the library, but we couldn't help pausing to watch the shadows of the flames dancing across the walls and ceiling. Sunbrook's ambiance was amazing. We managed to finish lighting the candles in all the rooms without any close encounters with Sharon. We were back at the table holding our cards when a shiny red Porsche pulled into the driveway and parked, followed by a forest green Audi. By the time we finished our game, several Jaguars, Range Rovers, BMWs, and one Rolls Royce graced the parking lot.

Guest book comments

"Thank you for making our wedding night even more romantic. The food and champagne were great!

Chapter 31

The guest's spirited voices and occasional jovial laughter resonated through the mansion. "It sounds like they're having a good time. I wonder if it's on Sharon's orders," Gwen said.

We both snickered into our cards before she added another ace to the three lying before her. It wasn't long until she had various three and four of a kind as well as straights spread across the table. She had won again.

I had grown weary of her winning streak and was about to suggest we take a break when I spied a tall dark-haired man bending around the door frame to look inside. He smiled at us and disappeared. A couple of minutes after we laid the cards aside and I grabbed us each a cola, he strolled in carrying a tray of sandwiches in one hand and a beer bottle in the other. A shorter sandy-haired gentleman, also carrying a drink, followed close behind.

"Hi, I'm Nate. I noticed you didn't have anything to eat, so John and I brought you sandwiches." He set the tray in the center of the table. "What are you playing?"

Gwen and I sat speechless, staring down at a pyramid of finger sandwiches. A bed of ruffled kale circled the base. Glossy red grape tomatoes decorated each ledge to the citrine star fruit at the top.

"I'm sorry for the imposition. We'll let you get back to your game," Nate said, misinterpreting our reaction.

"Oh, no! Please! You're not imposing. It's the sandwiches. Sharon would be upset if she found them here," I said, leaning against the back of my chair for a better view of the doorway, where I envisioned her charging through, fists in the air, ready to pummel us if she caught us with the contraband.

"There's a huge layout on every table at this party, plenty of food for everyone," John said. He picked off a tomato, "She won't miss these," and popped it into his mouth.

"This is a great house for a party. All the rooms are large making it easy to mingle. I know it sounds crazy, but the house glows with a warm, festive atmosphere, almost like it's enjoying the party along with us. Are either of you the owner?" Nate asked, pointing back and forth between us.

"Oh, yes. I'm Tiffany, and this is my sister-in-law, Gwen." I stood and offered my hand; each one shook it with a firm grip. "I'm the owner, and it doesn't sound crazy. Living here, I often feel Sunbrook's enchantment."

"Well, you have a beautiful home. Do you mind answering a few questions about the history?"

"Not at all," I said, but before Nate could get the first question out, my eyes averted to Sharon's short, stout figure that filled the kitchen doorway. Her eyes darted back and forth between us, as if assessing the situation.

"Gentlemen!"

They both jumped, sloshing John's drink. Amber droplets leaped over the side to disappear onto the matching grain of the Georgia pine. Both men turned their attention to Sharon for a moment and then brought it back to us. My eyes met Gwen's, and we both fought to suppress a smile.

"What are you doing in the kitchen? The party's in there," Sharon said, her head gestured toward the dining room.

"We're talking to Tiffany and Gwen," John said. "Tiffany owns this marvelous house." He looked around and gestured his hand in the air. "She's filling us in on its history."

"Come back to the party. The mayor is about to offer the Christmas toast."

"Ok, we'll be there in a minute," Nate said. He shot a glance our way and flashed us a silly grin.

"What the hell are my sandwiches doing in here?" Sharon hustled to the table and picked up the tray. She paused, turned her back to the men, and then put her face close to mine. Her eyes were slits and her mouth grimaced a silent warning before she turned around.

"Come with me now, gentlemen. You don't want to miss the mayor's toast." She marched across the threshold and disappeared around the corner.

"It was nice meeting you," Nate said, "We'll talk later."

"Yes, we'll be back," John added.

"No, they won't," Sharon barked from the hallway. "The party's in here."

Their voices faded into the hum of the other guests

before Gwen and I dropped back onto our chairs. We tucked our heads, and our hunched shoulders shook as we snickered into our palms.

"What a tyrant," Gwen said. "How about that shitty look she gave you. I swear she would have hit you if she hadn't been holding her precious tray of sandwiches."

"No, Sharon wouldn't risk it—not with Nate, a judge, and John, a wealthy philanthropist as witnesses."

"I'm flattered that such prominent people wanted to hang out with us. Do you think they'll be back?"

"I wouldn't be surprised. I would want to escape behind the scenes, too, if Sharon was the director on set. What a bully." I stood and walked to the fridge. "Gwen, how about I make some sandwiches?" My fingers motioned air quotes at the word "sandwiches."

Gwen laughed. "Sounds good, I'll put on the tea kettle." She walked to the sink and filled the kettle with water. "Then I'll beat you at another game of rummy."

We had just finished our game - Gwen won again - when John and Nate strolled in.

"Hey, we're back," John said and took a sip from his flute of bubbly liquid. He lifted his other hand and held out a flute for me to take. "Here, we brought you champagne." Nate handed one to Gwen.

"Wait a minute! Sharon would have a fit if she caught me drinking her champagne. I don't want to cross her, so I'll have to decline."

"There is no reason for concern. I supplied the champagne, so Sharon can't say a word. Here, take this." Nate pressed the flute into my hand and then poured both Gwen's and mine three quarters full. He raised his glass. We all followed suit. "A toast, to meeting new friends in this enchanting abode."

"Here, here," we all said, clinked our glasses, and drank. The pleasure of the chilled, smooth liquid on my tongue and the sensation of delicate bubbles flowing down my throat, made me close my eyes and savor the flavor of what had to be expensive champagne.

"This is delicious," Gwen said, swirling the sparkling vintage in her glass.

"I agree. I never tasted a wine so decadent before."

"What kind is it?" Gwen asked. She held up her glass to the light, furrowed her brow and examined it like a wine connoisseur. I giggled and gave her a gentle nudge in the side with my elbow.

"What? I'm doing it right. I've watched wine makers hold it up just like this on PBS."

"Yes, but you don't know what you're looking for."

We all chuckled and raised our flutes in unison.

"Cheers to wine makers," Gwen toasted, holding her drink toward us. Our flutes tinkled in song when they touched. Then we sipped.

"Cheers to wine connoisseurs," John said, his drink in the air. We clinked and took another sip.

"Cheers to PBS," I blurted, and everyone burst out laughing.

Nate set his wine on the counter. "Enough toasting! Let's play cards," he said, rubbing his palms together as he walked to the table, slid out a chair, sat, and started shuffling. "I'll deal first."

John joined him and waved us over. "Come sit." Let's try to get a game in before we're summoned again." Nate nodded in agreement while his lips moved, silently counting as he dealt the cards around the table.

We played, and I answered their questions about Sunbrook. Gwen discarded her last card, waved jazz hands over her head, and sang, "Rummy."

We threw our cards onto the table. "Gwen, you have won every game we played tonight," I said. "That's the last for me."

"You bet it is."

I froze at the sound of Sharon's voice behind me, my nerve ends tingled, raising the hair on my neck. The skin on my back crawled where her fingers brushed it to grip the back of my chair. My eyes whipped from face to face reading their expressions for clues of Sharon's next move.

"Sharon," Nate addressed her and stood. John also stood.

"We're having a chat with our lovely friends, Tiffany and Gwen."

"But the party's…"

"We know, the party's in there." He pushed in his chair, and they all started to leave. "Do you know the history of Sunbrook?" Nate asked as he followed Sharon.

"No," she kept walking.

"Well you should. It's fascinating." He looked back at us and winked.

Throughout the rest of the party, Gwen and I talked and later watched the guests pull out in their snappy chariots. The crowd had dwindled down until we heard only a few voices. Gwen and I turned our ears toward whispers outside the kitchen entrance. John leaned around the door jamb and set a bottle on the counter. Nate leaned around him and waved.

"Merry Christmas," John whispered, holding his pointer finger on his lips, waved "Goodbye", and disappeared.

We walked over and bent down to read the label. "Oh my god, it's Dom Perignon," I whispered. We both mimed clapping, dancing in place. "I'm hiding it in the pantry." I set it on the highest shelf and slid a liter of cola in front of it.

"Are you ready to start cleaning?" I asked.

"Don't you want to wait until she leaves?"

"No, if there's any issue with the rooms, I want to take it up with her right away." I gave Gwen a dry cloth and a large trash bag. "Check around for wet spots on the mantels and wood furniture and for smashed food scraps on the floor."

I directed Gwen to the music room while I did a quick sweep of the foyer. A pretty woman passed me in the library carrying a box of empty silver trays. Her long blond hair waved side to side as she leaned back to gain leverage. The heavy load stretched her arms straight; white knuckles gripped while she struggled to walk.

"I'll get the door for you," I said, rushing ahead of her. I closed it, looked through the window, and watched her pitch forward, almost falling when she set the box on the porch. She shook out her arms, pumped her hands open and closed, then rested the palms on her lower spine and arched her back. Two more women hobbled into the foyer burdened with more boxes. I slipped back and opened the door. At the bottom of the steps they set their heavy loads down and dragged them to the car. I'll bet this is the last time they help Sharon with one of her parties.

Champagne flutes formed a line on the table. All the other tables had been cleared, except for my tablecloths. Sharon slipped each flute into a slotted box, moving down the table, and sliding the container along with her. She had finished placing the last flute when the pretty blond entered the room. She flapped her hand at her and pointed to the box. The girl jumped into action, picking it up and carrying it out.

"That's it," Sharon said. "I'm out of here."

I followed her to the door. She stopped and waited until I scooted around her and opened it. She stepped onto the porch and turned to face me. She held a white envelope against her chest to show me my name written in elegant flowing script across the front.

"By the way, the guests left you a tip. She moved the envelope toward me but, when I reached out, she jerked it back. "But I think I'll keep it since you didn't follow my orders to replenish the food platters, and - your friend ate my sandwiches." My jaw dropped. "As well as cornered two of my special guests in your horrid little nook."She curled her mouth into a smirk, raised an eyebrow, and her eyes filled with loathing.

She opened her shoulder bag, but before she could place the envelope inside, it flew out of her hand and made a circle in the air above us before it dropped through a crack between the wooden porch and the stone threshold.

"Damn it," she snarled. "Well at least you'll never get it."

She turned and stomped down the steps headed for her car.

"You're right because it's on its way to hell where you can pick it up," I yelled after her.

Before she got into her car and sped out the driveway, she had shot me one more glare, and I could swear, I saw pitch forks fly out of her eyes.

Guest book comments

"Your magnificent home made for a pleasant weekend."

Chapter 32

My heart pounded, my blood raced through my veins, my skin and face grew hot. I lifted my eyes to the tall ancient trees that tended Sunbrook. Their stark, onyx branches waved against the twilight sky as if cheering me for my outburst that told Sharon "where to go." My arms reared up, and I yelled a resounding, "Yes!" then bowed to their majesty. A chilled breeze swirled under the portico roof and enveloped my body, encouraging me to get out of the cold. Gwen rushed toward me through the hall.

"I heard everything. Well done, girl. That's some moxie you showed there."

"Oh, telling her off felt good." My hand still gripped the knob. I slumped against the door and exhaled, dropping my shoulders, relieved that the party had ended and Sharon was gone.

"I'm curious. Let's count your tip. That crowd had some bucks." Gwen held up her hand and rubbed her fingers and thumb together.

"We can't, the tip's gone. Sharon threw it, and now it's trapped in a crevice in the stone foundation."

"Bummer!" Gwen's brow furrowed. She placed one hand under her chin and looked at the floor for a few seconds before she raised her head and straightened her back. "Come on! Let's at least take a look." She nudged me and opened the door.

"What?" I hung back. "Forget it. A stone foundation skirts the porch and there's no opening."

"What are you talking about? Here's an envelope with your name written on it lying on the step." Gwen let go of the door, and it crept open. Its hinges creaked.

"That's it! But I watched it…" A hint of Jasmine wafted past my nose.

"What?" Gwen asked, her eyes searching my face.

"Oh, nothing." I bent down over the envelope. "Thank you," I whispered before picking it up.

"Look, it's bulging." Gwen pointed at my hand. "It must hold a lot of money or it's all one-dollar bills, but I doubt that, given the affluence of the crowd that attended this party."

Our eyes met. "Dining room," I yelled.

Gwen shoved the heavy oak door. It slammed shut behind us as we dashed through the foyer to the built-in seat below the bank of leaded glass windows in the dining room. We sat Indian-style facing each other. I tore open the flap and laid it between us. My fingers trembled as I slid the one inch-thick stack of bills into view.

"Oh, my," I said. Thomas Jefferson's face lay before us. I moved it aside to reveal another. "How many twenties do you think are here?"

"Well, I'm not sure. Do you think maybe if we counted them we would know?" Gwen smirked. I counted off ten twenty-dollar bills. "Look, the next one's a Grant. You have two hundred and fifty so far." I paused to take it in. "Keep going." Gwen flipped her hand and leaned forward with her eyes glued to the pile.

I counted out twelve fifty-dollar bills. The next one sported Benjamin Franklin. We both caught our breath.

"Nine hundred dollars and we haven't reached the bottom yet." Gwen laid her hand over her heart. "The suspense is too stressful for me. Will you hurry up and finish counting?"

My frantic fingers grabbed the rest of the bills and flipped one onto another until the count reached thirty-three.

"Tiffany, tha…that's a total of $4,200.00. What a tip!"

We both squealed with excitement.

Then guilt replaced my elation. I lowered my eyes and dropped my shoulders, folding into myself.

"Uh oh! What's with the frown and why are you shaking your head?" Gwen ducked to look into my eyes forcing me to meet her gaze.

"Why would they leave me such a large tip? I didn't do anything to deserve this."

"They shared a great time with their friends in this enchanting atmosphere, and they're showing you their gratitude for making it possible in your elegant home." She waved her hand toward the room. "It's this place." She looked up and around at our surroundings. "It brings out the best in people, except for Sharon, of course. Money is their way of showing their appreciation."

"But so much money," I said breathless.

"Ok!" She slapped her knee. "They wanted to

outdo each other and, to prove they're top dog, they throw their money around." Her silly explanation revived my spirits.

"I want to share this with you for helping me tonight," I picked up the money and started counting.

"Stop," Gwen placed her hands over mine. "This is yours, and I don't want any of it. I came today to visit my favorite sister-in-law."

"I'm your only sister-in-law." I jumped up. "Let's celebrate. We'll break out the Dom Perignon, and you're staying the night."

Gwen leapt off the window seat, "I'll get the glasses." She started for the butler's pantry.

"Meet you in the library," I said, passing her on my way to the kitchen.

Gwen sat with her eyes closed in the burgundy wingback chair. Her feet rested on the ottoman. She had one elbow perched on the chair arm, with her palm facing up. She balanced the bowl of the goblet between two fingers and waited for it to be filled. I sat near her in the matching wing chair and set the Dom on ice on the end table between us.

"Let's give the wine a few minutes to breath before we pour," I said.

"You pour—I'm comfortable, and I don't want to move an inch."

The flames in the fireplace danced before us. The party candles in all the rooms were still lit. I sat quietly, taking in the ambiance of their glow that sent shadows to frolic about across the expansive arena. It appeared as if the walls were moving in time with them.

"Beautiful but kind of creepy, huh?" Gwen's voice broke the silence, and I flinched. "I'm sorry I startled you." Her hand cradling the goblet never moved. "Is the wine chilled?"

I lifted the Dom from its frigid crater. Ice maracas shifted then tumbled. Our private party had begun.

Guest book comments

"Great B&B! We appreciate historic buildings and are thankful for the opportunity to share your Sunbrook."

Chapter 33

My cheery mood matched the bright, eastern sun that spilled through the bedroom windows. With arms overhead, I arched my back and stretched until my toes tapped the filigree brass footboard. My lungs welcomed the wide yawn that overtook me. A slow exhale melted the tensed muscles, and my body went limp, sinking into the soft, pillow-top mattress. My hand slid back and forth across the Egyptian cotton sheets. I basked in their silky caress against my skin. I lay quiet to muse over the previous day—the attention and wine from Nate and John, my gumption to tell Sharon off, our party by the fire with Gwen and Dom, and my unbelievable tip. My mind envisioned the haphazard bills on my desk morphing into a neat pile, all paid and ready to mail.

I even told Gwen about Sunbrook's ghost after she grew tipsy from the champagne. "Nothing surprises me after the bizarre day we experienced." That was all she said before refilling her empty glass. I expected to hear her say, "I'm leaving, and I won't be back." I wonder if her outlook will change by morning.

I informed Mike about the generous tip when he came home.

"I'm not surprised. You're incredible." Then he kissed me on the cheek. "Goodnight," he whispered into my ear, sending a pleasant rush of warmth through my body

***

Grace sat at the table eating tomato soup and a grilled cheese sandwich when I entered the kitchen.

"That's your breakfast?"

"This is lunch. You slept through breakfast. Gwen said you both went to bed late. She left without any breakfast."

"She's gone already?"

"Yes, she said she's leaving and won't be back, and then she rushed out the door. What'd you do? Tell her about the ghost?"

"Yes, and she didn't have a problem with it last night, but I guess we did drink almost a bottle of wine by the time I told her."

I sat and filled Grace in on everything that happened. "And now, thank God, I have the money to pay last month's bills."

"That's not the first time you mentioned the bills. Is there a problem?" Her brow creased. Her eyes searched mine, waiting for an answer.

My scalp prickled with shame. Heat rose from my neck and crept into my cheeks.

"Forget I said anything. I'm going to clean the dining room." I stood and scurried from her worried stare.

"Wait, Tiffany."

I ignored her plea.

The dining room was spotless, and I discovered no evidence of last night's party in any of the rooms. After making my way back to the kitchen I stuck my head in the door. "Thanks Grace, you did a superb job cleaning up." I heard her distant, "You're welcome," as I escaped up the stairs.

Furious with myself for divulging our money problems, I paced across my room in frustration. "I'm not answering her questions, no matter how many times she brings it up." I covered my face with my hands. "Oh, I'm so embarrassed. How will I face her again? I shook my hands out and sat. "I'll stay here until the guest arrives. She'll be too busy to ask questions." My breath quivered as I inhaled and blew out the air. "I need to calm down." I took another deep breath, released and then another, repeating them while sitting cross-legged on the floor. My body began to relax as my eyes wandered to the hidden book and train case. *A distraction would help,* I thought.

I locked my bedroom door before pulling John Lloyd's journal from under the bed. My hands shook, making it clumsy to open the cover. I turned to the first entry.

April 15, 1912

The Titanic sank in the early morning hours. I'm waiting for news of my nephew and several friends and business associates who were sailing on her. The Altoona Chronicle reports that all have been saved.

My heart pounded at the mention of the Titanic.

May 7, 1912

The newspaper reports were false. Many perished when the Titanic went down. Ships are recovering bodies. The Marconi wireless I received, said three of my friends' and two of my associates' remains have been found. My nephew is still missing.

I paused, feeling his sadness resonate from the page. My fingertips trembled as they slid across his words. I longed for a connection to him and the times.

June 15, 1912

My sister, Louise, sent her daughter, Sarah, to live with us. She is unwed and with child. Her parents have disowned her. I don't know how they could since their son, Milton, had perished last April on the Titanic. Sarah is the only child they have left. I have consented to be her guardian until she becomes of age in six months. It's also when she's to give birth. She is a delightful child, and I have opened my home and intend to take care of her for as long as needed. My wife, Anna, agrees and has coddled her since she arrived.

December 26, 1912

Our family Christmas proved extra special with the addition of Sarah to our festive celebration. She has been welcomed and loved by all.

December 28, 1912

Sarah's Son arrived yesterday. Anna has taken over the care of the child until Sarah is well. She nearly died in childbirth. His name is Edward James Kelly, after his father, who had died on the Titanic.

February 3, 1913

Congress has ratified the sixteenth amendment. Next year we will be required to pay a federal income tax. I must find a way to hide my true income. My colleagues are also looking to do the same. Giving the government more taxes is revolting to us. We expressed, to no avail, that we already subsidize our fair share. Our lawyers and accountants have found few loopholes to avoid paying this new tax. I decided to claim a partial amount of my income. So there is nothing I can do but put the remainder of my cash away somewhere, but where? All financial institutions are obligated to report their customers' deposits to the government at the end of the year. So the bank is out of the question.

Intrigued with reading about another historical event and John Lloyd's personal dilemma, I read the next entry.

February 23, 1913

I had discovered a solution to my tax problem yesterday when I received a birthday gift from my son, a new LV steamer trunk.

September 11, 1913

Anna and I sailed on the Lusitania to Europe, a special holiday to celebrate our 40th wedding anniversary. We spent a month visiting Paris, Rome, and Madrid. We had a most enjoyable trip before we arrived at the docks in Southampton to board the Olympic, sister ship to the Titanic, and also her near mirror image. Anna grew apprehensive, and I had to reassure her during the whole crossing to New York, where we disembarked to board the train for Hollidaysburg.

December 27, 1913

I filled my old LV steamer trunk with the money, locked it and stored it in a secret place. I hid the key in plain view within a black leather bag among the bevy of keys to Sunbrook. It shouldn't be difficult to procure. It's the key with the purple velvet ribbon.

Guest book comments

"I had the best time at my friend's bridal shower! You were very hospitable, and the food was fabulous."

Chapter 34

I dropped the journal onto the bed beside me. My feet hit the floor and swept me across the room to the bureau. I stooped to my knees and pulled open the bottom drawer. A brass key, darkened with age, lay on the folded stack of lingerie. Its attached purple velvet ribbon complemented the luscious ruby of the wispy chiffon negligee. My fingers wrapped around the key. I held it up before my eyes then opened my hand, letting the ribbon loop over my ring finger, and the brass key rested against my palm. Jasmine aroma encircled my head as I examined the key.

"What do you know about this?" I asked the ghost. No response. "I'm on my own, huh? Well thanks a lot."

I remembered reading the initials J.C.L. engraved on one side when I found the lot of keys in the basement. I flipped it over and drew in a quick breath at the sight of the entwined LV initials. My mind went wild. *This could be the key to the steamer trunk John Lloyd wrote about in his journal. The attached purple ribbon, the initials, and the fact that it lay among Sunbrook's keys, they all correspond with his description. It's possible that he hid the money here. But if he did hide it at Sunbrook, it's been years. It's not possible that it's still here. Someone must have found it.* A knock on the door made me jerk.

I dropped the key onto the lingerie and shoved the drawer shut.

"Tiffany, Jack, the Dupont guy is here."

"Ok, Grace. I'll be right there."

I jumped up, looked in the mirror, and ran my hand over my hair, smoothing down the halo of rogue curls. Satisfied with the result, I opened the door and ambled down the stairs.

"Welcome, Jack. It's nice to have you as a guest again."

"Thank you. I like the peace and quiet here. I don't know what it is, but this place puts me at ease, and I feel comfortable. Almost like the house is glad I'm here." He touched his forehead. "Forgive me… I know that sounds crazy."

I slid a quick side glance at Grace to see her jaw had dropped and she looked at him as if he was daft. "You're nu…."

"On the contrary! You're not the first person who has told us that," I said, interrupting the criticism that was certain to come out of Grace's mouth. "Sunbrook is unique."

"You can say that again," she chimed in and rolled her eyes at me. She pulled Jack's overnight bag off his shoulder. "I'll take this up to your room while you check in." She turned and ran up the stairs.

"Come right back down, Grace. I need you in the kitchen," I called after her. She stopped on the landing, turned, scrunched up her face, and stuck out her tongue. My eyes averted to Jack. Thank goodness, he missed it. He'd been searching in his wallet for his credit card.

"Did you find the socks that I misplaced the last time I stayed?" He asked while signing his receipt.

I dropped my gaze to hide my shock at his question and pretended to look for something among my papers. "No." I searched through my mind to add something of reassurance. "But we didn't do a thorough search. We had assumed you'd find them in your luggage when you unpacked at home. Grace and I will keep an eye out for them."

"Don't put yourself out. I asked out of curiosity. You can discard them if they show up."

I'll bet the ghost already did discard the socks, I thought to myself

"Ok. You're in the Deborah room again, if that's alright?"

"Perfect," he said as he walked up the stairs.

Grace sauntered into the kitchen. "What did you want?"

"Nothing. I didn't want you pouncing on Jack in his room." I clamped my mouth, trying to hide my amusement.

"Believe me. I would like to pounce on him. He's hot!"

"Keep your voice down, Grace."

"Ah, he can't hear me. Not through these babies." She slapped the kitchen wall.

I shook my head. "Anyway, I'm going to the store for breakfast supplies. You leave Jack alone while I'm gone." I slipped on my coat and grabbed my handbag.

"Ok, I'll visit him when you get back."

"Forget it, Grace."

Her eyebrow raised and one side of her mouth turned up into a mischievous grin as she watched me close the door.

***

After Grace and I ate supper, we sliced fruit, readied the coffee pot, and set out the ingredients to bake fresh cinnamon rolls in the morning. We bid each other goodnight after we climbed the stairs to our rooms. I prepared for bed, then slipped under the covers to settle in, and read more of John Lloyd's Journal. The entries went on page after page about his bank, real estate, and street car businesses. Finally, on the last page he wrote about Sarah and her child.

December 27, 1913

Edward is one year old today. Since he is illegitimate, Sarah and Louise had planned a discrete family celebration to commemorate the event. Afterward, several of our colleagues, my son Henry, and I are traveling by train to Pittsburgh to meet with Carnegie and Mellon to discuss the federal tax laws and overseas bank accounts.

An overseas accounts! John Lloyd must have removed the money from the trunk and sent it to a foreign bank. It made sense, since he could add to it every year without the limited space of a steamer trunk. Disappointed, I closed the book and set it on my bedside table. I turned off the lamp, snuggled under the covers, and stared through the window at the stars glistening against an inky sky.

It was fun, at least for a little while, to think it possible that Sunbrook harbored a long lost treasure. Forget the mystery, Agatha Christie, and get to sleep.

You have an early day tomorrow.

Guest book comments

"Thank you for making our first B&B experience a most memorable one."

Chapter 35

The warmth of Mike's body against mine sent delightful sensations through my middle and beyond. My longing grew when I rubbed my hand down his muscular back and cupped his firm backside. Twenty-five years of knee bends, bicep, and core workouts while sanding and painting cars had kept his whole body toned. His breathing remained steady, so my touch didn't rouse him from his much needed slumber. I knew it wouldn't be fair to wake him. My bedside alarm would be ringing any second. Despite my reluctance to remove my hand, I rolled over and pushed the off button. I sat up and then paused to wipe the remnants of sleep from my eyes. I twisted back to Mike and couldn't resist reaching under the covers to give his full moon one more, gentle squeeze. Then I took a quick shower, dressed and primped, and went down the stairs.

The pan of cinnamon rolls sat rising on the counter. I arranged sliced oranges, kiwi and strawberries on the china plate, then placed a handful of plump blueberries strategically among the fruit for another pop of color. Once satisfied that it looked just so, I covered the plate with plastic wrap, set it in the fridge, and then pulled out the grapefruit juice to pour into a crystal pitcher. After arranging everything on the top shelf for quick retrieval, I filled a serving tray with one china, crystal, and silver place setting, a linen napkin, and a creamer and sugar bowl, then carried it into the dining room, and set the breakfast table. On my return, Grace popped her head around the kitchen doorway. My hand lost its grip on the empty tray at my side, and it clanged against the floor. I covered my ears while it wobbled around emitting a deafening clatter before it lost momentum as the noise faded. The tray lay motionless on the floor.

"Grace, why do you startle me like that? You know I hate it. My anger didn't subside so fast the last time, remember? And you told me you wouldn't do it anymore."

"I can't help it. You know, there is something about this house that makes me feel like…like I need to do it. After all, Sunbrook is unique." She tilted her head, wiggled her pointer finger into her cheek, and rocked to and fro, feigning innocence, then dropped her act, and straightened. "And it's a riot to see that surprised look on your face."

I blew past her to where I left the cinnamon rolls, but they were gone. I rushed to the oven and peered inside. The sugar, butter, and cinnamon mixture had started to bubble as steam escaped from the puffy dough.

"Yeah, I put them in the oven."

"I need a cup of coffee." I let out a long breath.

"Go sit down. I'll get it for you." Grace placed her palm on my back and directed me to the table. I dropped my shoulders and shuffled to the chair, plopped down and lay my face in my hands on the table.

"You need to lighten up, Tiffany, or this place will drive you crazy."

"No, YOU'll drive me crazy with all your shenanigans," I said into my hands. The click of the glass mug on the tile table brought my head up. I took a sip of the hot liquid. "But you're right, Grace, I do have to lighten up and not worry so much." I stared ahead as if in a trance.

"Tell me how I can help, and I will." She snaked her upper body within my view until I made eye contact. "I'll do double the work and do it faster, so you don't have to work so much."

"We'll see, Grace." I reached across and patted her on the arm. "But in the meantime, no more sneaking up on me, ok?"

"Ok, I guess I can give up seeing the scared face." She raised her brows. Her eyes grew wide as her mouth opened into a capital O. I burst out laughing. "See, see," Grace said, pointing at me, "You think it's funny too."

"You're hilarious, Grace."

"Oh yeah, and by the way, there is something I have to tell you."

The sound of Jack's footsteps on the stairs brought me to attention. "It will have to wait, Grace. It's time to fill the tray." We both scurried about the kitchen. Grace grabbed the fruit and juice and filled the coffee butler, while I pulled a piping hot cinnamon roll from the batch and slathered the top with dripping white icing. I scooped up the now full tray and, while walking out, turned around, and gave Grace a Cheshire cat smile, knowing she would relish in the job of serving Jack.

Jack finished his breakfast and went back up to his room. A few minutes later we heard him leave for work.

"I'll grab the breakfast dishes, Grace, but you'll have to finish cleaning up, I'm going to 2nd Hand Rose." I returned from the dining room. "Jack must have liked his bacon and eggs, he ate every bite."

"Yeah, the fruit, too! And he asked for a second cinnamon roll. He must have a raging metabolism." She dropped her head to look at her stomach and pinched the fleshy roll at her waist. I did the same with mine. "Unlike us," she said.

"Yeah," I agreed but noticed mine had turned into a mini roll since I've been eating smaller portions and had cut out late night snacks in the last few weeks.

I took the steps two at a time to my room. I wanted to freshen up before leaving, and I told Gwen I would be there fifteen minutes ago. After changing from my morning dress to a pair of black slacks and white cotton blouse, more appropriate apparel for 2nd Hand Rose, I bounded down the steps and through the kitchen.

"Wait, Tiffany, I didn't get to tell you."

"It will have to wait until tonight, Grace. Gwen's expecting me, and I'm late." I closed the door, jumped in my big ol' Cadillac, and drove off.

Guest book comments

"Tiffany, you have a beautiful and wonderous place. We'll be back!"

Chapter 36

Stacks of boxes overflowing with accessories and household items circled the consignment desk. Close by, along the wall, stood racks bulging with hung clothes tied into bundles, each with the consigners name and number attached. Gwen and Peg, one of our employees, hefted more boxes and clothes from the consignors waiting in line. Mobs of people showed up on Wednesday, one of the two days of the week when consignors could add up to twenty-five more items to sell without an appointment. Saturday was the other day, so we scheduled extra workers on both days to keep up. I threw off my coat, shoved my handbag under the counter, and joined in—grabbing clothes, tying them together, and adding the identification number. We kept this up until noon, when it tapered off. We ate a quick lunch and then emptied the racks before it would start to get busy again around two o'clock.

Gwen and I were the last to leave for the day.

"Gwen, I've wanted to talk to you all day. It's good we're alone now." I slid my arm into my coat sleeve. "Grace told me you won't come back to Sunbrook."

"She's right. I can't believe I stayed the night. The alcohol buzz had worn off by morning. I woke up and remembered what you'd told me. Fearing the ghost would materialize at any second, I got the hell out of there. I never dressed so fast in my life."

"The ghost is harmless. She's been helping me since she had made herself known. Who do you think retrieved the tip envelope from under the porch? I even think that she pulled it from Sharon's hand and dropped it through the crack, so that she couldn't take it. She's revealed secrets to me about Sunbrook and has given me comfort."

Gwen furrowed her brow and looked at me sideways. "Puh, how could a ghost comfort?"

"With a gentle touch—I've felt her hand on my shoulder like this." I reached toward her shoulder, but she flinched away. I jerked my arm back and placed the offending hand on my hip. "She also smells like jasmine," I added to hide my embarrassment.

Gwen shuddered. "There's no way I would find feeling the hand of a ghost comforting. I would be a screaming banshee."

"You wouldn't if you got to know her. Come tomorrow, and I'll introduce you. I know she'd like you. You've got charisma. She'll understand why you're my favorite sister-in-law."

"I'm your only sister-in-law." She smiled, and her gold-speckled brown eyes brightened as the lines between them disappeared. "You think I've got charisma, huh?" She raised her chin and turned her head in a haughty pose, displaying her profile.

I chuckled and waved her off. "Let's go home. High tea tomorrow at four—be there." I opened the door to a twilight sky dotted with the faint glow of yellow stars. They struggled to display their full glory through the last remnants of the sun's aura behind the purple horizon.

"Ok, but in case I get scared, set our tea table up by the door for my speedy exit. The banshee in me will also take over, so I suggest you supply your guests with ear plugs before I arrive." She waved, hunched her shoulders, then clutched her collar close against the frigid air, and dashed to her car.

***

While waiting at the pizza drive up window for our supper, my foot tapped on the floorboard in the anticipation of telling Grace about Gwen coming to meet the ghost.

Sailing down my driveway, I punched the button on the visor to open the garage. The door had lifted halfway by the time I passed under, hoping it would clear the roof. The old Caddy jerked forward then back in complaint when I jammed its sturdy shifter into park. The pizza box slid to the edge of the seat but my hand clamped down on the corner before it could tip over onto the floor. I jumped out and burst through the door into an empty kitchen. Disappointed that Grace wasn't there, I searched the other rooms that circled back to the kitchen.

Grace likes pizza as much as I do. She'll be down soon with her mouth watering when the savory smells of spices and melted cheese reach her room. Besides, she has to help me get the food ready for tomorrow morning.

My stomach growled, reminding me of my own hunger. I set plates, glasses, napkins, and a bottle of diet coke on the table for both of us and sat. The aroma of the warm comfort food relieved the tension in my body, and I leaned back to enjoy the tranquil view of Hollidaysburg nestled in the valley below.

A half hour had gone by and still no Grace. I decided to clean up and make the preparations for Jack's breakfast without her. Grace will be disappointed after he checks out tomorrow. She had tried to flirt with him before he left for work in the morning and when he returned in the evening. I even caught her stopping him on his way out for supper. Jack's not her only target—it's a sport for her to flirt with every handsome guy that comes through the door. I had explained to her that these men are too busy to stand around and be amused by her batting lashes and saucy innuendos. I wouldn't be surprised if Jack had tried to avoid her during his stay. He may even choose to stay somewhere else next time.

All I have left to do is set the coffee pot, and then I'm going up to her room to tell her about the pizza and about my fears that she could be chasing Jack away.

I turned out the kitchen light and climbed the stairs surprised to meet Grace on the landing.

"Where have you been? I brought you pizza for supper, and I thought you would be down to help me get things ready for the morning. Why are you dressed up?" My eyes took in her dangling earrings, fancy red dress, and black heels. "You look nice. Where are you going?"

"That's what I tried to tell you yesterday and then this morning before you left for work."

The door to Jack's room opened and we both

glanced up. He looked as handsome as ever in a red and white pinstriped dress shirt and black slacks. He stepped down to the landing and placed his palm against Grace's lower back. "Are you ready? Our reservations are for seven."

Grace winked at me and whispered as they passed, "You can start without me. I won't be eating pizza tonight."

Guest book comments

"This is a beautiful mansion, I wish I could live here."

Chapter 37

The hem of the ecru linen tablecloth kissed the rose, cornflower and aster bouquets woven throughout the rug beneath. White china dishes, edged in platinum, reflected the rainbow of color that glistened throughout the beveled glass within the wide oak door in the background. The main entrance to Sunbrook stood ready in case Gwen wanted to make a quick exit.

The clock in the foyer struck a quarter to four. She would be arriving soon. At least I hoped she would. The finger sandwiches, cinnamon scones, and chocolate and lemon petits fours arranged on the three-tier serving dish graced the center of the table. The kettle on the stove began to boil. I raced to the kitchen with my hands over my ears to muffle its shrill whistle. I flipped open the noisy spout and turned the burner on low to let the turbulent water drop to a quiet simmer. The corner of my eye caught Gwen's spiffy white Honda pull into a parking space. I poured the hot liquid over tea leaves in a china pot to steep then jogged through the foyer to greet her at the door.

"Welcome Gwen! I'm glad you came."

She stood in the doorway. Her saucer-like eyes darted back and forth around the foyer before she took a tentative step across the threshold. "Is she here? Where's the table? I don't see it. You promised you would put it near the door."

"I set up the table close to the front door, around the corner, at the other end of the hall. Come on in. Here, hold onto me." I offered my elbow, and she slipped her arm into mine. She hugged close and shuffled her feet as I pulled her in further. "Relax! She's not here yet. She'll arrive on the scent of jasmine." She watched my hand gesture graceful waves in the air. "Doesn't that sound like a lovely entrance?"

"I-I-I guess," Gwen stammered. She loosened her hold enough to bring back some of the circulation into my arm. I squeezed and released my fingers into a fist to squelch the feeling of needles in my hand.

"Gwen, I seem to remember that you told me you learned at your essential oils class that jasmine relieves stress and lowers blood pressure."

"I did?" She stopped and jerked her head forward, stealing a quick glance around the corner, before she jerked it back again. "Nice table," she said, with another slight release of her grip.

"Thanks! The tea should be finished steeping. I'll get it from the kitchen." I took a step, and she tightened her hold, pulling me back against her.

"You're not going without me," she whispered, wide-eyed, her face close to mine.

My eyes locked with hers, and the fear in them filled me with sadness, then empathy. "You're right, I'm not." I laid my hand on hers. "Hold on tight. We'll fetch it together."

***

With the teapot in one hand and Gwen wrapped around my other arm, we shuffled to the table. She still clenched me tight. I slid my chair close to hers, so she wouldn't pull me off of mine.

"I made chamomile tea to help you relax." I poured the steaming liquid into Gwen's cup.

She took a sip and closed her eyes. "Ahhh, delicious." She dropped her arm from mine, then chose a strawberry and cream cheese sandwich, and took a bite.

"Are you alright now," I asked?

"Yes, food makes me feel better every time." She reached for a cucumber sandwich and scone, adding them to her plate.

We were a half hour into our tea when a hint of jasmine caught our attention. Gwen reached into her pocket, pulled out a pill box, and opened the lid. Inside sat a small white pill. She popped it into her mouth, threw back her head, and with shaking hands gulped the tea until her cup was empty.

"Valium," she snapped shut the tiny case and dropped it into her handbag. "Oh, don't look so surprised! You knew I took it on rare occasions for panic attacks. Well, this is what I would call a rare occasion."

"She's not in the room yet. We'll know she's with us when the scent grows stronger," I had no sooner spoken when the glorious fragrance blossomed around us.

"Hello," the ghost's soft lilt danced across the room. "Gwen."

"H-h-h-hi," Gwen said. She raised her hand in a

wave, noticed it trembling, then fired it into her lap and covered it with her other hand. Her chest rose as she took a deep breath, held it for a few seconds, and then exhaled. Her shoulders dropped. The pill must have kicked in because she slumped a bit into her chair as the tension washed from her face. "I didn't want to come back after Tiffany told me about you, but she assured me that you were gentle and kind. By the way, thank you for helping her. As you can see," Gwen tilted her head my way and winked, "She needs all the help she can get."

The ghost's laughter resonated throughout the foyer. Gwen's jaw dropped in surprise before she burst out in laughter with her.

"Hey, what is this, mean girls?" I asked, feigning offense. Unsuccessful at suppressing my own amusement, I gave up and joined in.

"What's going on here?" Grace stood in the kitchen doorway, her hands on her hips.

Gwen and I stopped and stared at her.

"You sound like a bunch of banshees," Grace added.

My eyes locked with Gwen's, as we remembered her reference to banshees the day before at 2nd Hand Rose. We laughed even harder, holding our stomachs in pain.

"Holy hell, it wasn't that funny." Grace rolled her eyes, sniffed, then looked up.

"It's a private joke," I managed to say between breaths.

"You have a private joke that includes the ghost? Are you crazy? Wait," she held up her palm toward us. "Don't answer that." She started walking up the stairs. "You're all loony tunes." She looked to the air and yelled. "Including you, Casper," then she raced up the steps to her room and slammed the door.

"What was that all about?" Gwen asked.

"The ghost has enjoyed harassing Grace, so she yells at her and then hides."

"Tiffany, everybody knows that ghosts can pass through walls."

"Yes, but since the ghost has never entered her room, Grace considers herself free from any shenanigans there."

"Well, if you say so." Gwen said.

"Let's have more tea." I picked up the pot and poured. "Try the petits fours."

Our tea continued for another hour before Gwen looked at her watch. "I had better get going before my valium wears off. Let me help you clean up, before I go." She began stacking plates.

I carried the now full tray to the kitchen and set it on the counter; then I turned, surprised to see that Gwen had not followed. My ears pricked up at an exchange coming from the foyer. I moved closer to listen.

"I'm not afraid anymore. I know part of the reason is the valium, but I also think it's because our meeting has been a pleasant experience. I'm glad I visited Sunbrook today."

"Me…too," the ghost said in a hollow voice as her jasmine essence faded.

Cynthia Taylor Billotte

Guest book comments

"Lovely spot! Beautiful house! Great breakfast! Wonderful atmosphere!"

Chapter 38

I made my last impromptu ugly face of annoyance at our niece Jami's wedding reception. It had been a long, stressful day, spent getting everything ready, and now, I worried that all wouldn't go well. While putting the wine goblets in the cupboard in the butler's pantry, Cynde, my friend assisting with the reception, walked in from the dining room. "One of the guests would like a cup of hot earl gray tea."

The instant Cynde's statement hit my ears, I made the face thinking, *the large buffet set with coffee, liquor, beer, water, soda, ice tea, punch and lemonade wasn't enough! Now someone wanted hot earl gray tea!* For one whole second my cheeks raised enough to cause my eyes to squint and wrinkles to appear. The two vertical lines in the middle of my forehead deepened, and my lips disappeared into a thin straight line. Cynde's eyes grew wide, and her body grew ridged as she took a step backward looking like a trapped rabbit with no hope of rescue.

"That's okay; I don't want to bother anyone," I failed to notice a pretty, petite woman standing in the doorway. The guest with the request had followed Cynde to the pantry and witnessed the ugly face, too!

Without missing a beat, I smiled, "Oh, no! I can get you hot earl gray tea," I said, trying not to mirror Cynde's trapped rabbit stare.

The ugly face appeared a lot lately. Overworked with two businesses and trying to see that everything at the bed and breakfast was perfect, I felt my nerves were frazzled. My frustration at this complimentary wedding caused my mind to recall the exorbitant electric bill marked payment due lying on my desk. Plus exhaustion and self-pity have been my constant companions.

"I don't mind. I'll bring it right in", I said and retreated to the kitchen. My ego wouldn't allow me to apologize for my ugly face, so I just had to work to smooth it over because this tea lover wasn't just any guest. She was Adam's sister, Sherri. And because Jami did a short stint of exotic dancing in New York City, Sherri told her she wasn't good enough for Adam or his family.

Boy, did I mess things up for Jami?! I had to fix this now. I boiled the water, poured it through fresh, tea leaves into my best teapot and set it on a tray. After adding cream, sugar, sweetener, and extra china cups on saucers, I carried it into the dining room sporting my most kiss-ass face.

Five of the family members were sitting together at a table in the middle of the room. The rest of the tables were empty by now. The other guests moved out onto the porch to drink and dance. Lively rock-n-roll music and merriment resonated through the walls. I set the tea tray carefully between them and said, "I brought extra cups if anyone else would care for tea." I felt exposed and vulnerable but made individual eye contact, recommitting to resolving the situation. Willing my hand not to shake, I poured Sherri's tea, set it before her and waited for the recriminations to begin.

"When was the house built?" A young gentleman across from Sherri asked.

The house always gets them! I should have known their curiosity about it would divert the situation. "1896. Believe it or not it was what the wealthy called a summer cottage, built by the Lloyd family to escape the heat and noise of Hollidaysburg. The town was a hub of business and the railroad, with constant travelers and lots of steam engines passing through.

An older woman, she must have been Adam's mother, reached out her hand offering me a chair, "Please join us and tell us more about the house."

I sat, relieved of my vulnerability. "There is a brass button that was connected to a bell in the kitchen recessed in this floor, positioned where Mrs. Lloyd would dine. She would press it with her foot to inform the butler that it was time to bring in the next course."

"Interesting! You mean it's still here under the rug?"

They peppered me with more questions for the next half hour. I told them about the original wallpaper frieze and leaded glass china cabinets, the tile room in the basement and even the ghost. I was surprised at their friendliness. When the questions slowed down, I stood, "You're welcome to explore the guest rooms upstairs, and the third floor maid's quarters. I had a great time talking to you. If you'll excuse me, it's time for me to get back to work." I left the room feeling relaxed—I actually enjoyed myself for the first time today.

Later, after all the guests had departed, I overheard my sister, Deb, and Jami talking about Adam's mother and sister making fun of me during the wedding, something about my dress and a whale.

"What did you say?" I interrupted, walking into the foyer where they were standing.

Jami turned to face me sporting the trapped rabbit stare. "Several people heard Adam's family criticizing everything during the wedding and reception."

"Like what?" I said.

"It doesn't matter, they're always critical about something. That's just the way they are. Our wedding day was wonderful. Thank you so much, Aunt Tiffany."

I could tell by how she quickly dismissed Adam's family's rudeness and Deb's sympathetic look that they didn't want to hurt my feelings, so I let it drop.

"You're welcome, honey! I'm glad you're pleased, and I wish you forever happiness." I went back to the kitchen glad that Jami and Adam celebrated their wedding at Sunbrook, despite the electric bill. As for Adam's family, I decided my last ugly face was well deserved.

Guest book comments

"We loved every minute of our stay at Sunbrook."

Chapter 39

My arms grew tired from the weight of the Christmas gifts. I rushed to the dining room and set them on the table before any slipped from my hands. One more trip should do it. The Cadillac's huge trunk had been loaded with items from a shopping splurge that I couldn't afford, but I wanted this Christmas to be memorable. I latched onto the last seven bags, three of which were overflowing with spools of ribbon, wrapping paper, and large gold lamé bows. I added them to the table, shed my winter garb, put on a pot of coffee, and made myself a sandwich. Wrapping everything would be a huge task, but it was one that I relished. I imagined them arranged under the tree in the parlor, coordinating with its red, green and gold trimmings.

I finished eating, poured a mug of caffeine, walked back to the dining room, and turned on a Christmas CD. My favorite carol's glorious sound filled the room.

Do You Hear What I Hear?

I sat and listened with my eyes closed until the angelic choir finished with a giant crescendo.

A child, a child crying in the night,
He will bring us goodness and light.

I pressed the repeat button and then emptied all the bags, placing the gifts on the pile intended for each recipient.

It took me a couple of hours until the last gift, a sapphire and diamond pendant I chose for my niece, Corinne, lay on top the others. Its delicate bow shimmered under the twinkling white lights that embraced the tree. The colorful ornaments and lights among the cascading evergreens on the mantles, the warmth of the fire, and the festive music all intoxicated my senses. The mansion sparkled, prompting whimsical daydreams that replaced my nagging money worries. Our first family Christmas at Sunbrook would be magical.

***

A full guest docket and four holiday parties kept Grace and me busy for the next two weeks. Everyone raved about the beautiful decor and how the elegant rooms transported them back to a Victorian Christmas.

Now, with one day until my own celebration, it was time to prepare the food. I buttered and seasoned the turkey and set it in the fridge before whipping up a bowl of herb butter with honey. Then I made cranberry sauce and three trays of hors d'oeuvres. I opened the fridge and added them to the rest of the Christmas dinner—fresh bread dough, ready to rise and bake with the hot appetizers before our family arrives. I checked the last item off my list as the clock in the foyer chimed four. I took a deep breath and let it trail out until my lungs emptied. My muscles relaxed, and I basked in my accomplishments while listening to the regal melody of the Westminster chimes.

Mike would be home at five-thirty as he had done every Christmas Eve since we've been married. My plan was to enjoy a relaxing evening before the fire. I draped a plush faux fur blanket over the settee and ottoman then ran upstairs to shower.

The kitchen door knob's screech and the creak and moan of the steps under the weight of boots announced Mike's homecoming. I pressed thin blotting paper between my berry-red lips, released it with a "Mwah" and then air-kissed my reflection. I sprang from my vanity bench to strike a pose in my new, red satin pajamas.

"Tah-dah," I sang when he opened the bedroom door. "You like?"

He leaned back, eyebrows raised as he took in my ensemble, from my Santa hat to my fuzzy reindeer slippers. "Cute," he said, grinning.

"Good! Because we're matching tonight." I directed my hand to the bed where an outfit lay in his size.

"You expect me to wear that? What if someone sees me?"

"Grace is staying at her parents' home tonight, and there are no guests. We're alone until our family arrives for supper tomorrow. Besides, you won't mind after a couple of beers." He tilted his head and shrugged. "Come on! It's Christmas, a time to loosen up and get cute with me."

"Ok, I'll wear it… but without the hat."

"Great, meet me in the parlor. I'll stoke up the fire and will have roast beef sandwiches and beer waiting for you." I pumped my brow with a side glance and smiled, "And later, maybe a few other nibbles." I threw him a kiss. "Now, don't be long, dear."

I left him standing at the bed rubbing the luxurious satin between his large, rough fingers as he mumbled, "I can't believe I agreed to this."

I popped my head around the foyer door to get a peek at Mike coming down the stairs. He had stopped halfway and turned to look behind him.

"Hey, tough guy, whadda ya looking for?"

He jerked back around at my voice, his eyes wide with surprise. Then he furrowed his brow and looked back over his shoulder as he took a hesitant step down.

"I thought you were behind me."

"Nope, not me."

"What's that smell?"

"Jasmine. Ready for a beer?" I held up the open bottle like a torch.

"Well, you overdid it with the air freshener."

The satin shirt fit snug showing off his muscular chest and arms. "Mmm," I murmured and fanned my face with the dish towel I was holding. He smiled and shook his head.

"Don't be such a drama queen! I know I look silly." He continued down the stairs and at the bottom grabbed the brew then pulled me against him, capturing my lips in a lingering kiss. He released me and took a swig of his suds. My chest rose and fell as my breath came in short bursts. I felt certain my palm, cold from his drink, would sizzle as I pressed it to my hot cheek. I felt powerless for a moment or two before gaining my composure. Our eyes met and his ocean blues crinkled at the corners when he grinned at my reaction. He raised his finger and flicked the fuzzy white pompom at the end of my hat. “How’s that, Santa baby?”

Guest book comments

“Exquisite house with ambience. Hostess Tiffany—very charming.”

Chapter 40

"One more mantel to clear, and we're done," Grace said as she added another full box of decorations to the dozen that littered the foyer. "Whew, what a job! Do we have to carry all of this back up the two lo-o-ng flights of stairs? Why don't we stuff it somewhere down here? How about the butler's pantry or the garage?"

"Come on, Grace, think of it as a good workout. It'll knock off the few pounds we gained over the holidays." I pulled the hem of my top down over my hips. "We won't have to try and hide our recent bulges that have appeared."

"Hey, we had to overindulge when sugar and carbs called from every corner of this party house for the last two months. And weren't you still baking cookies yesterday?"

"Yes. I've decided, this year, to welcome guests by placing a plate of homemade cookies in their rooms before they arrive."

"Good grief," Grace threw up her hands. "You get any more welcoming, and they'll never leave. They'll think you're their live-in maid. I'm giving you fair warning." She gestured her thumb toward the door. "I'm outta here if that happens."

Ignoring the threat, I walked past her, opened the elevator door, then snapped the lid tight on the plastic container, and set it inside. "There, we can stack four at a time and ride up to the second floor, take them off, and ride back down. It eliminates carrying them up one flight. Are you happy now?"

"I will be if you top off the boxes with a half dozen cookies to take to my room."

I shook my head, "Come on, Grace. Let's get these loaded."

We rode the elevator to the second floor and then lugged the decorations to the storage space one flight up.

***

I settled a crate against its twin in the third floor storage room. "Thank God, that's the last one."

"I'm whipped," Grace said, fanning out the front of her shirt. "I need a shower."

"Go ahead. I want to tidy up around here." I lied. John Lloyd's journals lay waiting for me in the secret room. Sunbrook's walls talked through them. Its history revealed with each turn of a page. I hid my wringing hands behind my back, eager to get rid of Grace, so I could retrieve one.

"You bet, but come down in a half hour. I'll have coffee and cookies on the table by then."

"Cookies!" I placed my hands on my hips ready to reprimand her.

"Oh, relax! One of the bookings for tomorrow canceled their trip. They won't be eating them, so we might as well." She raised her chin and crossed her arms in front of her, "So there." Then she mocked a salute and hustled out the door and down the stairs.

I listened for her bedroom door to click shut, then

pulled the flashlight from its charger on the wall, and tiptoed down the hall. The latch that held the little door tight flipped up without effort. I opened it about a foot and squinted into the blackness of the hidden room and shuddered. The flashlight had let me down the last time leaving me terrified in the dark with the ghost.

What's wrong with me? I tell everyone else they don't have to be afraid of the ghost, and I stand here in fear of her now. Get a move on girl! That journal is your link to Sunbrook's past.

Thinking of it gave me the courage to step inside. With my arm out straight before me, my hand felt for the dangling light string. Then I remembered the flashlight at my side.

"Dah," I whispered and pressed the button. My eyes crossed at the string suspended two inches from my face. I gave it a gentle pull, but nothing happened, so I jerked on it a couple of times, but the bare bulb on the ceiling remained dark. Then, with a gentle touch, I twisted it tight.

"Damn it. It's blown." I lifted the flashlight. "You're all I've got, so don't you go out."

The circle of light framed the cardboard boxes. "All you have to do is get in there, grab one and get out." I rolled my eyes. "Yeah, all ya gotta do." I let out a long breath and stepped forward, crossing the room. With the box lid raised, I reached in and grasped the book on top, then turned to exit.

"Wait. Here." The ghost's muffled voice stopped me in mid-step.

"Oh no, not again, I've got to get out now. I may

lose my light." I charged through the little door and turned back. "I'm sorry," I said before latching it behind me.

I slinked to my room and slid the journal under the bed. Then lingered under a muscle-soothing hot shower and dressed, before leaving to meet Grace. The comforting smell of rich coffee wafted around me at the top of the stairs. My body shivered. There was a chill in the air. The thermostat on the wall beside me read sixty degrees. My finger pressed the up arrow to raise the temperature until the furnace kicked on. The display read sixty-six when Grace yelled up to me.

"Hey Tiffany, the furnace won't come on—I think it's broken."

Guest book comments

"Thanks for this beautiful mansion! It helped make our first wedding anniversary a great one."

Chapter 41

I sprinted down the stairs. "It can't be broken! We have guests arriving tomorrow afternoon."

Grace stood in the kitchen doorway. "Well, it can and it is broken."

"I'm calling furnace repair."

"Hey, tell them to send Dan—he has a nice butt," she yelled as I rushed past her to my office.

My hands shook so hard—my fingers kept missing the numbers on the keypad. With a strained voice, I convinced the company to send someone within the hour. Relief ran over me as I hung up the phone.

"They'll be here soon, Grace." She sat at the table cradling her cup in both palms. I poured my coffee, sat across from her, and snatched a cookie from the dish between us. I dunked it in the hot liquid and took a huge bite. Before swallowing I devoured the rest. I grabbed another one, dunked, and shoved the whole thing into my already full mouth.

"Slow down! Your cheeks are bulging. What are you doing, foraging for winter?"

I threw back a gulp to wash it all down and pushed the plate toward Grace, then backed my chair away from the table. "I'm not even hungry. I'm stress eating."

"Stop fretting, Dan will fix it." She bit into a

cookie. "Mmm, these are tasty. The guests will enjoy them—if there are any left."

I jumped up. "Drop it, Grace. We have to light all the fireplaces right away."

"I say we wait and watch Dan light them." Grace grinned and wiggled her eyebrows up and down.

Ignoring her humor, I started with the fireplace in the foyer. By the time I finished lighting the last one, the furnace company's white van pulled into the driveway with Dan at the wheel.

"Yes!" Grace said throwing her fisted hand into the air. She leaped out of her chair and ripped open the kitchen door. She watched Dan removed his toolbox from the back of the van then turned to face me. "Nice view, huh?" I rolled my eyes, and she snickered. He approached her at the door. "Hi Dan," she said, in a voice dripping with molasses.

"Hello," Dan said. He focused his eyes on hers and leaned away sideways as he passed.

"She's harmless, Dan. But I'll walk you to the cellar door. Sit, Grace," I hissed, narrowing my eyes when she moved to follow us.

When I returned, Grace had vacated the kitchen, so I sat alone with my coffee and waited, praying that the furnace would come to life again.

***

Dan handed me the yellow copy of the bill. I dropped it on the table averting my gaze from the total.

"I got it started again, this time, but you're going to have to replace that dinosaur soon. We can install a new furnace that uses half the energy with twice the efficiency."

I looked down and fought back tears as I walked toward the door to see him out. Gathering all my resolve, with my hand on the knob, I faced him. "Alright, Dan, install it as soon as possible."

"I'll put the work order in right away. We'll be here next week. I'll give you a call with the day and time."

I opened the door, but a goodbye was caught in my throat—all I could do was nod my head when he stepped out onto the porch. His eyes filled with concern. "Take care," he said and turned to go.

I closed the door and darted into my office to lock the world out. Then plopped onto the chair, put my face in my hands, and burst into tears, releasing all the pent up tension. I cried until I was spent, then wiped the tears, walked to the wall mirror, and stared at my reflection. My ruby-rimmed eyes shined with the liquid remnants. Angry red blotches covered my cheeks and neck. Longing to get to my room and lie down, I peeked out into the foyer and heard Grace rattling dishes as she loaded the dishwasher.

I scurried to the kitchen doorway. "I'm going upstairs to take a nap, Grace." Not waiting for a reply, I clutched the railing and pulled myself up. My arms wanted to give out as my feet grew heavy with each step.

I collapsed onto the bed and stared at the ceiling. I loved Sunbrook, and the thought of losing it brought despair. A long sigh escaped my lips and my body lay limp as hopelessness engulfed me. My eyelids grew heavy, and I welcomed the oblivion of sleep.

***

The trees outside my window cast long shadows across the ceiling and down the walls. I rubbed the sleep from my eyes and watched the shape of their craggy limbs fade away as dusk invaded the room. I sat up, dropping my legs over the side, and turned on the bedside lamp. The radiator pipes creaked as hot water moved through them. The furnace had turned on, reminding me of its borrowed time.

"Oh Lord, please help me." My simple petition spurred a shimmer of hope inside me. Positive thoughts and one day at a time came to mind. My body unfurled, and my back straightened. The stance brought me renewed strength.

I walked to the bathroom sink and splashed my face with water, then gazed into the mirror. Water dripped off my eyelashes and chin. Its coolness felt refreshing and brightened my mood. Wrinkles appeared at the corner of my eyes and mouth as I smiled. "Thank you, Lord."

I filled my lungs with air and let a long breath escape my lips. Shoulders dropped as muscles relaxed and my mind cleared. Then my eyes grew wide at the memory of the journal beneath the bed. I whipped the hand towel from the bar on the wall, rubbed it across my face, and let it fall into a heap at the bottom of the sink. I rushed to the bed, pulled out the journal, then flopped cross-legged onto the mattress. Holding the book with one hand, I caressed the linen surface as my fingers slid over the cover. Then I opened it to the first entry.

January 25, 1914

I corresponded with Sarah's parents informing them that she missed them and would like to return home with their grandchild. They responded that "Sarah is welcome but not the illegitimate child." I revealed their sentiment to Sarah. Of course she refused to go without her son, but she has become melancholy in recent days.

January 30, 1914

With the intention of lifting Sarah's spirits, I've commissioned a photographer to travel to Sunbrook for a sitting with Sarah and Edward. The meeting in Pittsburg with Frick and Mellon, as well as our lawyers, gleaned several solutions for hiding a handsome percentage of our profits from the government.

January 31, 1914

I've convinced Sarah to visit her parents alone. Her presence may soften their resolve, and they may welcome their grandson. The photographs of mother and child were delivered today, and they are charming. It brought Anna and me much joy to witness Sarah's glow when she cast eyes on them. I bestowed them on her to secure in her valise for Boston.

I skimmed over the next two dozen pages of bank reports. One entry divulged Lloyd's accountant's creation of two sets of books, the first to show to the government and a private set to record his flourishing business.

February 21, 1914

Anna and I are traveling to Pittsburg to attend Henry DuPont's son's wedding two days after Sarah's departure. I told Anna to acquire a nanny. Sarah had rejected the commission in the past.

March 1, 1914

Sarah boarded the train for Boston at dawn. Edward cried all day. Anna heard the nanny yelling at him and gave her a reprimanded. I informed Anna that the nanny is professionally trained to handle the child and instructed her not to interfere.

March 12, 1914

I delayed my return home from the office. Edward has become unruly and disruptive. I told the nanny to gain control of the boy or face dismissal. My anticipation for our trip has grown in avoidance of our turbulent abode.

March 15, 1914

Edward has been calmer, so we instructed the nanny to bring him to the parlor. I fear we have been too indulgent these past two days. His attachment to us has become overwhelming. He cries when Anna gives him to the nanny to retire to the nursery. He misses his mother. I'm rethinking my act to encourage Sarah to leave him behind.

March 16, 1914

Anna instructed our butler, Jeffries, to dismiss all the staff for the weekend, except the cook and the kitchen maid. Jeffries and the nanny would also stay on.

March 17, 1914

Our train arrived in Pittsburgh at noon. We dined with the DuPonts at their mansion.

March 18, 1914

After the wedding, we received a telegram from

Jeffries that Master Edward is missing. The police had been called. I telegraphed Sarah instructing her to come home but did not divulge the news of her son.

March 19, 1914

We departed Pittsburgh on the morning train. The nanny had vacated before we returned to Sunbrook. The police informed us that Edward had died. Jeffries had found him in the attic, locked in the room at the end of the hall. His little battered body lay just inside the door beside an overturned child's chair. A multitude of scratches on the inside of the door revealed that the nanny had locked him in the dark room alone more than once. I'm sick with remorse for instructing her to discipline the child or be dismissed.

March 20, 1914

Sarah returned to Sunbrook today. She went into hysterics when we told her about her son. Anna held onto her, escorting her to the parlor where he lay in his coffin. Sarah lifted him into her arms and has been holding him and wailing for hours.

March 21, 1914

After much difficulty, Sarah relinquished her child to be laid to rest in Sunbrook's family cemetery.

March 24, 1914

I telegraphed Sarah's parents today. The gardener had discovered beautiful Sarah among the Jasmine vines along Sunbrook's north wing. She had jumped from the widow's walk. The note on her pillow read that she wished to join her son. May God have mercy on her soul.

March 28, 1914

Today Anna and I depart for our home in Hollidaysburg. My wife affirms she will never return to Sunbrook.

I closed the journal. What a tragedy. My heart broke for this family. My tears moistened the parched linen cover. Jasmine wafted about the room.

"Are you Sarah?" I asked.

"Yes."

Guest book comments

"The most exquisite B&B we've stayed at, peaceful and lovely."

Chapter 42

"Oh Sarah, the anguish of losing your son must have been too much to bear."

"Guilt."

"You had no reason for guilt."

"Left…Him."

"But you left to fight for him."

"Alone."

"No one could have predicted the outcome. You were leaving him with his family. You thought he would be well cared for. The nanny is the only one who is to blame for Edward's death and your aunt hired her, not you."

"Should…Have."

"You had no control of the situation or any reason not to trust your aunt's decision. Your train left before the nanny arrived."

"Guilt."

"Oh Sarah, it's heartbreaking. I had no idea that my beautiful home was the scene of the murder of an innocent child and the death of his loving mother. I had wished that Sunbrook's walls could talk, but in this case it's difficult to listen. I don't mean to presume how you should have felt. Please forgive me."

"Forgiven." Sarah whispered and her fragrance lifted from the room.

The journal grew heavy in my lap. I wanted to be free of the burden of emotion for a while, so I tucked it far under the bed.

The radiator pipes creaked and groaned as if struggling to stay alive as well as prompting me to tell Mike about our dwindling savings account, the Lloyd journals, and the ghost. He wouldn't be home for a couple of hours, so I scanned the room for a mindless chore to fill the time. My gaze landed on the messy vanity. I dove right in uncluttering and rearranging the drawers, cleaned the mirror, and dusted the top. Then stood back and admired the arranged vignettes of sparkling crystal perfume bottles and jars of creams and powders. Satisfied with the results, I showered and donned my pajamas, then sat up in bed, pulled up the covers and waited.

The pages of the glossy magazine fluttered in my trembling hands. I leafed through it front to back then back to front, mulling over in my mind how to explain our dilemma to Mike. A half hour later he entered the room and flashed me a smile.

"Wow, what more could I ask for, to find my wife in bed waiting for me when I come home after a long day at work, although, I would prefer without the flannels. You could sweeten the surprise and remove them while I shower."

"You're in a randy mood tonight." I forced a smile, dropped the magazine in my lap, and slid my trembling hands under the covers at my side.

"I had a good day at work." He unbuttoned his shirt, shook it off, then balled it up and did a slam dunk into the hamper. His t-shirt and pants followed.

Then he slid off his socks and leaving them bunched up, landed them with the others. "I finished replacing the convertible top that was giving me so much trouble on that '69 Olds I was telling you about. Now it looks perfect and works on cue."

"That's good news, but I'm not surprised. You've always been a master with cars."

"Aw shucks," he said, with a sheepish smile.

While watching him saunter into the bathroom, I decided it was a good night to tell him everything. I pulled off my pajamas bottoms as he closed the door behind him. Then lifted the top over my head and tossed it to the foot of the bed. I snuggled under the covers and listened to the shower handle screech in protest before the burst of water spray pounded the porcelain and echoed off the tile walls and floors, all sounds of comfort to me.

Minutes later he opened the door, and I lifted my head to look. He stood in the doorway with a towel wrapped around his waist. His eyes dropped to my pajamas lying on the covers. He unfastened the towel and let it fall, then leaped onto the bed and rolled on top of me. He held the blankets tight against my body, trapping me within a shroud of protection, hope, and love.

***

We lay spent in each other's arms after our passionate lovemaking. Our dewy skin glistened in the moonbeams that streamed across our bodies through the tall window.

"Are you sleepy?" I asked. My head lay on his chest.

"No, it will take me a while after that vigorous workout."

I huffed a quiet breath and smiled. "I'm wide awake, too." I rose up on my elbow. "We have to talk."

He lifted his head and met my eyes, "What about?"

"We have to replace the furnace. It's a big house, and everything but the radiators will need replaced. Dan said it will lower the heating bill, but it's going to cost the bulk of our savings.

"Who's Dan?"

"The furnace repair man. Mike, I'm worried. It will take at least three years for the business to make a profit. What if something else goes wrong? There is no way to replenish the savings and, if we run out, we could lose Sunbrook."

"How much will it cost?"

"Twenty-five thousand dollars."

"What!"

I dropped onto my back, squeezed my eyes shut, and clamped my palms against my ears.

He shot up, his face close to mine. "I knew we couldn't afford to buy let alone maintain this mausoleum. It could ruin us! Why did you have to keep harping on buying it when I told you that I didn't want to move? You were selfish and didn't care what I wanted. You wanted Sunbrook!"

His venomous words spewed against my face. His hot rapid breath exploded across my skin.

"I know! I know! I know!" My voice creaked between sobs. I opened my eyes to face him. Tears trailed from the corners and puddled at my ears. His labored breathing slowed, his black pupils shrunk, and the ocean-blue of his eyes that I treasured returned and they softened.

"Oh, God," he lifted me into his arms. "Tiffany, darling, I'm sorry. I shouldn't have lost my temper and yelled at you like that." He rocked me, his cheek caressing my temple. My stiff muscles relaxed as our bodies bonded together, in love.

Guest book comments

"What a wonderful place. We're glad to be back."

Chapter 43

With my eyes still closed, I shook off the clouds of dreams as I slid my palm over the mattress. Mike's spot felt cool. His body warmth would have risen not long after he did. I rolled to the edge and lay face to face with the clock that told me he had left at least an hour ago. My thoughts wandered to last night.

"I'm ashamed of yelling…I didn't mean what I said." He told me. "You are the most considerate person I know. I wanted Sunbrook, too. I'm here. You don't have to take this on alone. We'll figure it out together. Tiffany, you're everything to me."

I rolled onto my back and wrapped my arms around my body remembering his strong embrace holding me close as I drifted off to sleep. My heart throbbed with love for him. Bliss filled my soul, and a prayer rolled off my lips. "Please bless my husband today! Thank you, Lord! Amen."

Grace's slippers scuffed across the vestibule from her room and stopped outside my door. I waited for her knock but then heard her steps continue until they were muffled by the carpet runner on the stairs. My stomach growled, looking forward to the hardy breakfast Grace would prepare. By the time I had dressed and wandered through the guest rooms to make sure they were spotless, I caught a whiff of bacon laced with fresh brewed coffee. My mouth watered in anticipation of the delectable feast. I raced down the stairs and into the kitchen just as she cracked the last of four eggs onto the griddle beside six slices of sizzling bacon. I rubbed my palms together eager for a taste.

She turned the eggs over. "Hand me a plate," she said, pointing the spatula to the end of the counter.

I grabbed both plates. She filled one, handed it back, and took the other. I sat at the table where slices of buttered toast lay on a paper towel in the center. Grace joined me as I took a big bite of egg and nibbled on a slice of bacon like a bunny eating dandelion leaves.

My jaw froze mid-chew when I looked at Grace's face. She stared at me with her eyebrows raised.

"What?" I mumbled.

"Tiffany, are you okay?"

I nodded.

She shook her head back and forth. "You're stress-eating again and last night, while on my way downstairs for a late night cookie snack, I heard Mike yelling. What's wrong? Trouble in marriage paradise?" She asked, with a smug half-smile and hooded eyes.

My surprise, then annoyance, followed by anger must have shown on my face because a scarlet blush started at her neck and rose above her wide eyes into her hairline. She dropped her head and stared at her breakfast.

I lingered over a sip of coffee and simmered, watching her squirm. "You think our marriage is a joke? Well, I'll not put up with your comedic improve. Do it again, and you're out. Got it?" I said in a raised, firm voice.

"Yes," she whispered, her head still down.

I stood and picked up my mug and plate. "Oh, and stay the hell out of the guests' cookies!" I stormed out of the kitchen and through the butler's pantry to the dining room. I dropped my breakfast on the table with a clatter. Coffee droplets splashed onto the oak surface. I pulled a cloth napkin I had patted into a neat fold for my guests out of the buffet drawer and sopped up the mess. Then dropped onto the chair and started eating as fast as I could until the plate was clean, before downing the lukewarm coffee and slamming the empty mug onto the table.

"Damn it, a good morning ruined," I growled.

The scene that brought on my foul mood replayed in my head. Why would Grace scoff at me and my marriage? It's sacred to us, and anyone criticizing our relationship in any way is an intrusion. I'm surprised because Grace had never tried to hurt me and stood defensive when anyone else attacked me in any way. Regret for the way I spoke to her started seeping through to my gut. I know now that I blew up because of my own insecurities about our marriage, my lingering guilt for letting Mike down, even though he reassured me that we both caused our financial dilemma.

The corner of my eye caught Grace's appearance in the doorway. She took a tentative step toward me, so I turned to face her.

"Tiffany, I want to apologize for my obnoxious behavior. I acted out of envy for you and Mike. I've never experienced, with anyone, the special and intimate bond that you both have."

"It's all right, Grace! I understand now and accept your apology. We won't mention it again."

"You got it," she said, with a breath of relief. She started to back away while pointing up. "I'm just going to hop up to my room for some R&R before we're overrun with guests."

"Go ahead, I'll check them in. I'm going to sit here for a while. Oh, and Grace, you'll need a snack—help yourself to some cookies." She left the room and my mind wandered to last night and Mike's tenderness and understanding.

Resolve to do my part overwhelmed me, and steps to a solution entered my thoughts so fast that I grabbed a pen and paper from the buffet drawer and started a list. As soon as I finished, I cleaned up my breakfast dishes and headed for my office. I wrote up ads on the Sunbrook website for Victorian teas, garden parties, a Mother's Day breakfast, and old fashioned ice cream socials. Then I laid out the plans to hold a Day Spa. Clients would be pampered with massages, facials, body masks, manicures, and pedicures. After a haircut and style, a cosmetologist would do makeovers, and then a photographer would take a glamour photo for them to remember and share, spreading the word of their incredible experience. If the first one was a success, I would take reservations for two days each month thereafter. I decided to later add workshops held by health professionals and life coaches.

I sent out emails to the local wellness and beauty

businesses asking if they would like to participate, and then created a pamphlet to distribute to women's clubs and organizations, libraries, restaurants, retail stores and hairdressers.

Sunbrook's elegant and enchanting décor and grounds were the perfect setting for my ambitious enterprise. It would take a lot of work but should generate several thousand dollars per month. Optimism replaced my defeatist outlook.

Guest book comments

"From the spacious room to the comfortable bed and delicious breakfasts, staying at Sunbrook has been wonderful, and we will recommend it to others."

Chapter 44

"Grace, a guest, Diana Clayton, is arriving this afternoon for a three week stay."

"Oh yeah! She visiting family or something?"

"Probably not, she lives in Altoona and is the employee manager at Sears."

"A big wig, huh?"

"No, Grace. An employee manager is not a big wig, so please don't ask her."

"Sounds like a big wig to me," she said under her breath.

"Anyway, it's a beautiful day, and I'm going for a walk. If I'm not back in time, check her into the Carrie Ann Room." I escaped through the foyer door then closed it to muffle any protest from Grace. I breathed in the fresh spring air and set out for the path to the forest behind the house. I meandered around the playhouse John Lloyd had built for his children. The large Victorian structure, constructed of the same yellow brick as the mansion, featured six tall windows stretched nearly to the gingerbread trimmed eves. I cupped my hands against the sun's glare and looked to the one end at a fancy fretwork fireplace and a wooden toy box. Child-high, built-in cupboards lined the wall at the other end. I'd been too busy to visit the playhouse since we moved in, but there was no time for a proper visit today either.

I headed for the forest.

The narrow path threaded through the towering trees twisting and twining every few yards as if to hide a secret around the next bend. In some places exposed roots of the century old trees had slowed my gait in order to avoid tripping over them. I rounded a curve and came upon a small clearing of hallowed ground—The Lloyd Pet Cemetery. Two strips of iron forged with a rough weld to form a cross rose above the weathered wooden signs inscribed with beloved pet's names—Rex, Beasly, Bella, Squeaky, Gensyn, and many more—set in three long rows. I sat on a low stump before them and mused about children running around Sunbrook's yard with a ginger and white collie, sitting and stroking a fluffy white cat, and small gentle hands cupped around a silky blond hamster. My imagination brought the pets to life in scenarios of companionship and bliss before following the path back to Sunbrook.

A Volvo sat parked in the driveway. I trotted to the kitchen door and entered to find Grace setting up the tea cart. "Did you invite Diana to our four o'clock tea?"

"Of course and she'll be there. I had finished baking the scones." She opened the oven and pulled out a tray. "And this is the last batch of the cookies."

"Great! I'll wash up and make the sandwiches"

"I'll cut the crust off the bread as soon as you put them together, but you do all the fancy-smancy arranging on the plates. You'll want them perfect, so I'm sure you don't want me to do it."

"You're right. I don't—perfect is not your forté."

It was close to four when I placed the last sandwich on the tray. I ran upstairs to freshen up and on my return found Diana and Grace in the dining room. "Here she comes. Tiffany can answer your questions about the history better than I can. I'll go heat the tea."

***

The clock chimed four just as Grace entered with the tea. In the next two hours Grace and I learned that Diana was starting divorce proceedings and needed a place to stay. She saw my ad and decided a bed and breakfast would be more comfortable than a hotel. I gave her free range of the kitchen and downstairs rooms if she wanted to have any guests and the liberty to use the washer and dryer. We became good friends in the three weeks that she stayed. She met Mike and found him reserved but friendly. I told her he often doesn't show his feelings. And that his head is filled with work and cars.

The second week of her stay, she introduced me to Jerry, her friend and co-worker, a handsome man with his sandy blond hair, deep blue eyes, and charming smile. He was friendly and would stop to talk a few minutes with Grace and me on his way upstairs for a visit with Diana or when Diana came down with him to show him to the door. Grace's eyebrows rose every time he went up to Diana's room. I think they had an understanding because he never stayed longer than an hour or so. He struck me as a kind and caring person, and he seemed to adore her.

The third week of Diana's stay was coming to a close. We decided to have breakfast together for her last two days. We knew we would miss each other. I stepped out of my room to the scent of lilacs filling the air. The morning sunrays broke through the stained glass windows on the staircase throwing bursts of color all around me. I walked through them watching the spectrum wash over me, the staircase, and then the foyer as I made my slow descent. Diana stood at the library doorway. She closed her eyes, lifted her nose in the air, and smiled as she drew in a deep breath. I joined her and noticed three vases of lilacs in the room.

"Oh, how lovely, Jerry brought you lilacs," I said.

"Jerry didn't bring them. The lilacs were here when we came down."

"Then who…?

"Look! They're in every room." I followed her to the dining room where a bouquet sat in the middle of the table and two on each end of the buffet. She hooked her arm in mine and pulled me to the music room where a vase sat on the table beside my reading chair as well as one on the center of the mantle. The tall delicate blossoms overflowed into a graceful drape with the mirror behind capturing their full beauty in its reflection.

"There's a vase on the kitchen table too. Mike must have brought them," she said.

Tears filled my eyes blurring my vision. "He must have picked these at our other property. It's near the garage where he works. I had planted eight bushes there years ago and would cut them every spring as soon as they were in full bloom. I also had mentioned to him last month that to my surprise there weren't any lilacs at Sunbrook. But it's not like Mike to do something so romantic. Plus, it would have taken him time to cut them in the dark after work and then fill the vases and place them in all the rooms. He would have been beat. I'm surprised he had the energy. This is the most romantic thing anyone has ever done for me." My heart swelled with love and pride for him, and I added, "You know Diana, Sunbrook has changed people, but I never thought it could change Mike."

"How romantic, you're lucky to have a husband like him. He's special."

"He's perfect." I said, reflecting on the small declarations of love he has shown throughout our marriage. The admiration with a touch of envy in Diana's eyes pulled me from my reverie. I saw how the thought and the experience of the lilacs gave her joy. I was happy to share it with her. "If you'd like, you may pick one for your bedroom."

"Really" she said? Her eyes sparkled with delight as she looked around to choose.

"Sure, I want you to enjoy them, too."

"Alright, how about this one?" she picked up a white vase and swept it out in front of her, reminding me of Ella's grace and charm in the movie *Enchanted.*

"A lovely choice," I said.

"Excuse me, Tiffany, but I can't wait to put these in my room."

I sat on the antique settee to relish in Mike's loving gesture. Then I smiled, bound up the stairs, and selected a mini chiffon negligee from the drawer. I held it up to admire on my way to the bed and spread it across the cream satin comforter. The pale color under the gauzy fabric made the royal purple appear even more luscious—then, the finishing touch, an added sprig of lilac, of course.

Guest book comments

"Tiffany, thank you for sharing the lovely intricacies of your decoration talent; we enjoyed our sojourn in the Victorian era. You are a lovely hostess."

Chapter 45

"Welcome to Sunbrook. I'm Tiffany, your hostess." The attractive couple before me resembled models for a posh hotel in a travel magazine—he in a lite blue Polo shirt and navy pants and she in a blush-pink floral chiffon mini dress.

"Hello. I'm Travis, and this is my wife, Emma." She flashed me a smile revealing a perfect line of sparkling white teeth surrounded by full glossed lips. The smile reached her bright blue eyes, crinkling them at the corners. Her long golden curls bounced as she and Travis walked further into the foyer. Their eyes grew wide at Sunbrook's opulence.

"Wow, this is some place," Travis said with Emma looking up and around, her jaw slack, nodding in agreement.

"Let me show you around. On your left is the music room."

"The walls are covered in velvet," Emma said, gliding to the center of the room. Her full skirt flowed as pink patent kitten heels pivoted, while she gazed at the crystal chandelier above. "It's like standing in a music box."

As I watched her, my heart swelled at her wonder. I glanced at Travis. His eyes, set on her, radiated admiration. He went to her, laced his fingers with hers; their eyes met, and they leaned into each other as if scripted.

"Come, I'll show you the library."

"Look Travis, the *Titanic*." Emma pointed to the pair of inverted glass paintings of the Ship, one sailing toward the iceberg, the other floundering while surrounded by lifeboats full of survivors.

"They were painted in 1917 to commemorate the fifth anniversary of the Sinking," I said.

"Emma and I have been fascinated with the *Titanic* since we saw the James Cameron's movie. When we read the story about your collection and the Bed and Breakfast in the *Altoona Mirror* and then watched your interview on the news, we knew we had to meet you."

"I'll be happy to show you the full collection and chat over tea after you're settled. Here is the dining room, where you'll be having breakfast. I think you'll recognize the plate in the shadow box on the far wall."

Still holding hands, they walked mesmerized into the room and stood in front of the shadow box. "It's a *Titanic* First Class dinner plate," Travis said.

"The Wisteria pattern," Emma added.

"Yes, it's an actual plate used in the filming of the movie."

"This is so cool," Travis said, looking at Emma. Wide-eyed and speechless, she just nodded.

"Come, I'll show you to your room." I smiled at their reaction to the plate, remembering my same amazement when I first laid eyes on it.

Travis grabbed their bags in the foyer, and they followed me up the stairs gaping at the six framed original 1912 newspapers, all with headlines of the Sinking and its aftermath.

"This is your room." I opened the door and stepped back. "I took the liberty of placing a TV with a DVD player at the foot of the bed. Stacked beside it is every *Titanic* movie ever made, some are in black and white. My favorite is *A Night to Remember.* It's based on the personal accounts of the survivors."

"How kind of you to do that for us," Emma said. "Travis, we can have a movie marathon and in such a beautiful room. Oh, there's a fireplace." She leaned her head to the side, laid her hand on her heart, and sighed, "How romantic."

Guest book comments

"Our weekend at Sunbrook was a dream come true. We felt like royalty in our elegant room and eating our delicious breakfast in the glamorous dining room."

Chapter 46

"Mm, I'll never grow tired of that fragrance. It's comforting to know you're here, Sarah." I pulled the light string and averting my eyes, crouched past the sad little chair, and then shined my light on the stack of boxes where the journals lay.

I crossed the room and lifted the last two books from the top box. After shifting them to the crook of my arm that held the flashlight, I placed the empty container on the floor. I opened the flaps of the next one and peered inside. Four more diaries stood side by side with their spines facing up. Before I could examine them further, the books on my arm somersaulted in on top of them. The flashlight followed, all landing askew with the beam pointing at the ceiling.

"What the... Sarah, did you hit my arm?" She didn't answer. "Why would you do that?" I asked, assuming she was guilty. While retrieving the light, a hard push sideways threw me off balance and knocked it out of my hand again. It landed with a loud thump but didn't go out. My feet scrambled over each other as they fought to keep me upright. My shoulder slammed against the wall. I bounced off and fell. The force propelled me across the smooth floorboards to the middle of the room. A dull pain throbbed against my scalp. I reached up and discovered a lump where my head had hit the floor. I crawled to the light and sat, overcome with dizziness.

I leaned back against the boxes and closed my eyes, concentrating on taking slow, deep breaths to quell the nausea rising to my throat. I opened my eyes, picked up the light and laid it on my lap. My body relaxed and my head lobbed to the side in the direction of its beam. My hand flew to the painful lump, when my brow creased at seeing a hidden door in the wall, hanging wide open. It must have been knock open when I hit the wall. Still unsteady, I crawled to the opening and peered in, sweeping the room with the light. The beam caught something large against the far wall. I inched forward to get a better view.

Particles of thick dust cast an eerie glow as they danced in the circle of light. The object grew larger and took on a rectangle shape. Now a few feet away, I could see that it was a huge brown chest with three brass latches. I moved close and ran my fingers over the rough embossed leather. The light, now smaller but brighter, revealed a tan pattern against the brown background. I leaned closer and squinted, waiting for my eyes to adjust to the light. My vision cleared enough to read the entwined initials LV repeated in a pattern across the surface.

"It's the steamer trunk that matches the set of designer luggage I had found weeks ago."

"Yes," Sarah whispered.

My heart raced. I pressed the spring loaded button on the latch, but it refused to open. I shined my light on and around the trunk and then scoured the rest of the room looking for the key.

"Damn, no key. Maybe it's stuck." I rose to my knees, gripped the sides of the lid, and shook it, hoping the latch would jimmy loose, but it wouldn't budge.

"Sarah, do you know what happened to the key?"

"Yes."

My heart raced. "Please tell me where to find it."

"Your…room."

"What do you mean my room? Why would I have…? My jaw dropped at my quick intake of breath. The floating dust in the air flew into my mouth, coating my throat. A fit of coughing followed. Each inhale between coughs pulled in more dust. The walls closed in as I struggled for air. I crawled from the room and ran into the hallway. I bent forward hacking and gasping, my hands on my stomach and throat. My gag reflex sent spasms of pain through my core. I stumbled into the bathroom, praying for water. It had been awhile since the sink here had been used. My fingers squeezed around the porcelain handle and twisted. The fixture resisted. Panic sent a wave of adrenaline through me. I gripped it with both hands and turned with all my strength. The faucet gurgled, and then burped air and spurts of brown water before turning to a steady stream. I cupped my hands under the rusty water and gulped the precious liquid. The stale taste slipped over my tongue to flood my parched throat. The water cleared, so I splashed my face and rubbed my grimy hands together under the flow.

"I've got to get that key." I plugged the flashlight

into its charger, crept down the stairs, and then crossed the vestibule in hopes of avoiding the Shipleys.

"Damn! I'm busted." They stood on the staircase landing. "Pardon my appearance. I'll clean up, and we'll talk *Titanic*."

Their eyes lit up. "Oh, that would be wonderful," Emma said.

I closed and slumped against my bedroom door. My eyes drew to the lingerie drawer. I tiptoed over and knelt before it. My hands shook as I opened it. My breath caught. The key with the purple velvet ribbon lay nestled on the delicate fabric. My body trembled with excitement. I reached for the key but stopped mid-air. My shoulders drooped in disappointment at the thought of the Shipleys waiting for me. I sighed and closed the drawer then stripped, showered and dressed before reapplying my makeup.

Travis and Emma still stood on the landing, now taking turns reading portions of the *Titanic's* sinking aloud to each other.

"This headline says the captain shot himself on deck," Travis said. They looked at each other, their brows lifted.

"That's one eyewitness's account," I said walking toward them down the steps. "Another told reporters he encountered him in the water after the ship went down. So no one knows for certain where or how the captain died."

"Fascinating," Emma said.

"Yes, and sad because he was set to retire as soon as he returned from this voyage, it says here." I pointed to a paragraph on the newspaper. "You two take your time here and if you have any questions, I'll answer them in the library where the rest of the collection is on display. I'll go prepare the tea and meet you there."

They both held open a book, reading to each other again, when I set tea and scones on the table. We spent the next two hours examining the collection. Their wide-eyed interest at every item fulfilled my desire for comrades in all things *Titanic.*

"What time is it?" Travis asked, looking at his watch. "We better get going, Emma, we have reservations for supper in twenty minutes. Thank you, for your time and for sharing the *Titanic* with us."

"Oh, yes," Emma said, breathless, then hugged me on tiptoes before she tucked her hand under Travis's arm. She squeezed against him, returning his loving gaze, and they departed through the portico door.

When it clicked shut behind them, I darted up the steps, two at a time.

Guest book comments

"We don't ever want to leave Sunbrook. Being within its walls felt like a hug. Thank you for sharing your collection and knowledge of the Titanic. It was a night to remember!"

Chapter 47

"What's the rush, Lover Boy on his way home?"

I jerked to a stop at Grace's voice from across the vestibule.

"No, just on my way to finish rearranging things upstairs," I said, avoiding her stare. "Um, after I tidy up my room." I side-stepped to my door and grasped the knob, then jumped when she pushed her door, letting it slam shut. "Need any help before I leave to visit Mom?" With one eyebrow raised, she tilted her head sideways and grinned.

"No, you go ahead, I'm sure she's eager to see you."

"Yes, she adores me." Grace flung open her arm, placed her hand on her chest, and lifted her nose in the air. "And I'm taking her out to supper for her birthday."

"Well, tell her happy birthday for me." I backed into my room, closed the door as she passed, and then opened it a crack.

"Tidying up her room my ass! Lover Boy will be here any minute," she said on her way down the stairs.

I went to the window and watched her get into her car and disappear down the driveway before racing to the drawer and pulling it open. My insides quivered at the sight of the key. I snatched it off my favorite black negligee and ran out. The door at the end of the hall stood wide.

I grabbed the flashlight, entered the passageway and stood in front of the steamer trunk. My fingers massaged the key against my palm. Learning a lesson from my earlier fiasco, I lifted the front of my shirt collar over my mouth and nose against the dust and whispered, "This is it, Lord! Oh, please let it be there." I knelt and directed the key into the hole. It fit snug like the last piece in a puzzle. I turned it to the right. The latch clicked and then sprung open. My breathing quickened as my heart thumped against my chest, its beat pounded in my ears. I reached my arms out further and pulled down the other two fasteners on the front, and then taking a careful breath, I lifted the lid.

A heap of papers and business envelopes spilled out onto the floor. "Oh no, more papers!" My shoulders dropped along with my hopes. I went limp, resting on my heels. Tears welled up and spilled down my cheeks. "I should have known I wouldn't have been lucky enough to find any money, but why would John Lloyd hide a trunk full of papers in here?" I picked one up and shined the light over it.

Seventeen sacks of flour…………..$23.00
Twenty cartons of eggs……………$12.30
Thirty sacks of sugar………………$18.50

"A list of household groceries no less!" I snatched up several more and leafed through them. "These are all the same, damn it, why would he keep these?" I yelled up at the ceiling, then crumpled the papers in my fist, and flung them into the air. My body shook as my anger grew; and with one arm, I swiped the mound of pulp back and forth out over the sides. Now exhaustion and frustration replaced anger. I dropped the light into the trunk, lay my head and chest on the remaining contents and sobbed.

Soon the tears subsided. I forced my upper body onto my elbows, and squeezing my head between my hands, glared down at the light. The beam fell on a drawing of an eye peering up at me. I moved some papers aside to get a better look and revealed a portrait of a man, along with the number 1,000. Anticipation radiated a tingling sensation through my scalp to the tops of my ears. I uncovered the rest to discover it to be a one thousand dollar bill. My frantic shoves whipped any remaining papers onto the floor. I froze. My eyes scanned across the unbelievable sight. Tears pooled at their rims. I smoothed my hands over a neat layer of crisp bills, wrapped with paper bands. Then grasped a bundle in each hand, hugged them to my chest and squealed.

Before placing them back in their slots, I spied another like them underneath. I lifted that one out and saw another under it. I pulled out the next two layers and still more followed. Tears spilled over and streamed down my cheeks as glee bubbled up through my chest to my throat, then burst out, racking my body with hysterical laughter. I hugged my stomach and stumbled out to the hallway, away from the dust that my uncontrollable joy had kicked up around the trunk. My fit of laughter and crying continued, as I rolled on the floor with my knees up, still holding my middle. Minutes passed before I gained control and lay on my back, spent, with my arms spread.

Then my reason returned, "I have to call Mike!" The thought of him enveloped me with happiness. I smiled and relished in the feeling for a few seconds, then jumped up, and scurried to the trunk.

"Oh, God!" I prayed as I looked down at our incredible windfall.

Exhilaration and gratitude overcame me. My hands shot up toward the ceiling, fingers spread wide. "Thank you!"

Guest book comments

"I am fortunate to have found your historic home. Sunbrook was a nice alternative to a traveling fool. I hope to return again to enjoy your hospitality and the setting."

Chapter 48

The hinges moaned and the lid resisted closing, as if disappointed to return to its dormant state. I pushed down harder until it relinquished and shut with a *whoosh.* Dust motes rushed through the light beam. I hooked the front of my shirt over my nose again and backed out of the room with eyes fixed on the trunk, anxious that it might disappear if I looked away. Jasmine filtered through my make-shift cotton mask, reassuring me that the money would still be here when I returned with Mike.

"Thank you, Sarah. I couldn't have found John Lloyd's treasure without you."

"Call…" Her commanding voice echoed through the rooms, "Mike!"

I made a swift exit sprinting down the two flights to my office. My hand shook as I dialed the garage. "Mike, can you come home, now?"

"Now?"

"Yes, I have something to show you."

He chuckled.

"Yes, that, too!" I said, pleased by his response.

"I'll be there as soon as I put the tools away."

"Ok, hurry. I'll wear my black negligee," I added.

"Mm, my favorite," he breathed into the phone.

As soon as he parked, I ran out to his truck and jerked open the door. He slid off the seat with his hands covering the front of his work pants.

"Is there anyone here who can see me?" He stood close in front of me poking his head around at the windows and the grounds. Then his amazing blue eyes looked down at me. "I'm excited just thinking about you in your lacy ribbons and bows."

"Later." I laughed and cocked my head toward the portico door while pulling on his hand. "Come on! This is almost as good."

He followed me through the door and up the stairs.

"Wait, where are we going? We passed our bedroom."

"Upstairs. Hurry, Grace or the Shippleys could come home at any time." I held onto his hand as we climbed the narrow stairs to the third floor hallway. He spied the open door.

"In there? Come on, Tiffany, I prefer the bed." He leaned back, grasping my hand with both of his to pull me in the opposite direction, but I resisted, so he let go.

"Like I said, this is almost as good." I grabbed the flashlight on the way down the hall. "Follow me… and watch your head."

"Normally, I'd follow you anywhere but…" He shrugged his shoulders. "Oh, what the hell." He slipped his fingers into the back of my waistband and bent over, trailing through until we stood in front of the trunk. He dropped his hand from my waist to caress my backside and whispered into my ear, "What do you want me to do now, beautiful?"

"Look." I lifted the lid and pointed the flashlight

inside.

The fragrance of jasmine swirled around us.

Guest book comments

"We find ourselves grateful for Sunbrook, where quietness and hospitality are a gift to these travelers."

The End

About the Author

With a mastery of an Altoona Writer's Guild member and expertise of a *Titanic* memorabilia collector, our debut author lures us to the enchanted world of Sunbrook Mansion Bed and Breakfast and takes time to unveil its elegance and beauty, its breakfast smells and mysterious jasmine fragrance. Her style is calm and soothing even when trouble and deep secrets are unfolding. Her main characters are everyday people with big dreams and big hearts.

Cynthia lives in Central Pennsylvania with her husband, Mike and their manx cat, Jacob and two tuxedo cats, Twilight and Jasper. They have an adult son, Michael.

Made in United States
Orlando, FL
01 October 2022

22893741R00147